Irish Fairy Tales

Sinéad de Valera was married to the former Irish President, and died early in 1975 at the age of ninety-six. She wrote several books of Irish fairy tales for children. In this selection of twelve stories Mrs de Valera tells of witches and wizards, poor boys and younger sons making their fortunes, wicked stepmothers, and princes and princesses being rescued.

All the stories have an element of fantasy, and all are original yet steeped in tradition.

Also by
Sinéad de Valera
More Irish Fairy Tales

Irish Fairy Tales

SINÉAD DE VALERA

Text illustrations by
Chris Bradbury

**MACMILLAN
CHILDREN'S BOOKS**

The stories in this collection were selected from *The Emerald Ring*,
The Four-Leaved Shamrock, *The Magic Girdle*,
The Miser's Gold, *The Stolen Child* and
The Verdant Valley by Sinéad de Valera,
published by C. J. Fallon Ltd, Dublin
This collection published 1973 by Pan Books Ltd
This edition reprinted 1995 by Macmillan Children's Books,
a division of Macmillan Publishers Ltd
25 Eccleston Place, London SW1W 9NF
and Basingstoke

Associated companies throughout the world

22 24 26 28 30 29 27 25 23

This collection © C. J. Fallon Ltd 1973

ISBN 0 330 235004 4

Printed and bound in Great Britain by
Mackays of Chatham PLC, Chatham, Kent

Contents

The Captive Princess

Years and years and years ago, when Fionn MacCool in Eirinn and Fionn Gall, a brother giant in Scotland, were building the Giant's Causeway, which was to run between the two countries, there lived in a glen in Antrim a young man named Hugh.

Everyone liked Hugh. He was very kind and neighbourly and it made him sad to see anyone in pain or trouble. He had also a great love for animals.

All the people in the place where Hugh lived had heard of an unhappy princess who had been carried off by a wicked giant and was kept a captive in his castle. This castle was a crannog or lake dwelling. It was built on stakes of wood driven down deep in the earth in the centre of the lake. The giant's wife was a witch and if anyone attempted to cross the lake, she set the water in motion and caused it to form whirlpools so that neither swimmer nor boat could reach the castle.

Hugh had a great desire to rescue the princess, whose name was Maca. One day he was sitting in his little house when he heard a wailing sound outside. He went to the door and saw a dog limping by, whining pitifully. He brought the dog into his house and saw that there was a large thorn in one of his front paws. He extracted the

thorn and bathed the paw. The dog tried to thank him by
licking his hand and then seemed to show that he wished
Hugh to follow him. He led him some distance from his
house and then turned down a narrow lane with high
hedges on each side. At the end of the lane was a tiny
little house. An old woman was sitting at the door. She
looked very sad but when she saw the dog her face
brightened. She thought he had been lost, he was so long
away from her. The dog ran forward and put his head
in her lap.

'I found this dog outside my house,' said Hugh. 'There
was a thorn in his paw and when I took it out he seemed
to wish me to follow him.'

'Good man,' said the old woman, 'and good dog. He
wants me to befriend you as you have befriended him.'

Now this old woman was a *bean feasa* (a woman of
knowledge), that is, a woman with magic powers and
with knowledge of things distant and hidden. She talked
with Hugh for some time and he told her of his desire to
rescue the princess.

'It is a hard task,' said the old woman, 'and there are
many dangers in the way, but you are strong and
brave and you will succeed if you follow my directions.'

She went into the house and came out again with a
large shell in her hand. Stretched across the shell were
silver cords, something like the strings of a lute or violin.
The old woman touched the strings and Hugh thought
the music was the sweetest he had ever heard.

'Take this shell,' said the old woman. 'You will come
to the Valley of Weasels. They will rush to swarm around
you and attack you, but touch the strings lightly and they

will become harmless. You will then come to a dark, dense wood through which it will be impossible to pass. Again, touch the strings and all will be well. Next, you must cross a deep, rugged quarry, but at the sound of the music your way will be clear. You have a long journey before you and you will need food.'

Again she went into the house. She returned carrying a large oat cake.

'Take this,' she said, 'and my blessing with it.'

'I shall never forget your kindness,' said Hugh, as he set off with a stout heart.

It was not long before he reached the Valley of Weasels. They rushed towards him as if they would spring at his throat. Hugh drew his fingers across the strings of the shell. Immediately the weasels formed a line on each side of him and as he continued to play they marched along with him till he passed out of the valley.

Next he came to the wood. The trees were so high and so close together that it was impossible for him to pass through. Hugh sounded the strings and all at once the branches parted and the trees themselves seemed to follow him till he came to the far end of the wood.

At last he reached the quarry. There were great jagged rocks on each side and a hollow in the middle. When he began to play, the stones from the bottom rose up and formed a smooth path for him and those at the sides moved gently with him till he reached the farther end.

He now sat down to rest near a clump of sloe bushes. As he was eating his oat cake, a tiny little bird fell from a robin's nest in the bush. He rose at once and gently placed the fledgling back in the nest.

Suddenly a little man stood before him. He had bright, twinkling eyes and a very friendly smile. He handed Hugh a feather, saying as he did so:

'For this your kindly deed
As on your way you speed,
Take this and in your need
'Twill serve you well.

'By the side of the water which surrounds the giant's castle you will see a seagull. Strike the bird with this feather.

'Now haste away,
Make no delay,
E'er close of day,
All will be well.'

Having said this, the little man vanished.

Hugh continued his journey. After a time he again sat down to rest and eat some more of the cake. Just above him was an old oak tree with ivy climbing along the trunk. A bat had in some strange way got entangled in the ivy and could not move and there it remained, with the glaring sunshine hurting its poor eyes. Hugh climbed up the tree and placed the bat on the shady side, hidden by the ivy and protected by the branches of the oak.

Again he heard the words:

'For this your kindly deed,
As on your way you speed,
Take this and in your need,
'Twill serve you well.'

There stood the little man, handing Hugh a bat's wing. 'If you turn this around three times in your right hand, darkness thick as night will fall about you. This darkness will last for a short time only.

'Now haste away,
Make no delay,
E'er close of day,
All will be well.'

Like a flash the little man was gone.

When Hugh had travelled for some time, he sat down on a stone by the roadside. From the other side of the hedge came a sound as if some creature were in pain. He went through the hedge to the place from which the sound came. There he saw a cat down in a deep well and unable to climb out. Hugh took off his coat and, leaning over the edge of the well, lowered it towards the cat. Puss caught it with her forepaws and Hugh dragged her to safety.

'For this your kindly deed,
As on your way you speed,
Take this and in your need,
'Twill serve you well.'

There stood the little man, handing Hugh a cat's eye. 'Take this,' he said, 'and if you hold it in front of you, the darkest way will become bright and clear before you.

'Now haste away,
Make no delay,
E'er close of day,
All will be well.'

Again the little man disappeared.

Hugh journeyed on. After a time he came in sight of a huge stone castle built in the centre of a lake. This he knew to be the giant's home. At one of the top windows he caught sight of a beautiful, sad face and he knew that the Princess Maca was a captive there.

As Hugh came near the castle he saw the giant and his wife standing on the steps. When the pair saw Hugh, the giant waved his club round his head and the woman raised her wand over the water. Immediately it foamed and turned in all directions and formed whirlpools all round the castle.

Hugh felt it would be impossible to cross that dangerous lake but just then he saw perched on the bank beside him a beautiful seagull. Remembering the little man's advice, he struck the seagull with the feather. All at once the bird became so large and strong that Hugh mounted on its back and was carried across to the castle. When he descended from the back of the bird it flew up into the air.

The giant and his wife rushed down the steps but Hugh waved the bat's wing and in the darkness the pair lost their footing and fell headlong into the water. The whirlpools dragged them down, down, and they were never heard of again.

By the light of the cat's eye, Hugh ascended the stairs to the room where the Princess Maca was. As he reached the door, the darkness disappeared and Hugh turned the key which was on the outside of the lock.

Maca told him she was the daughter of the King of Ulster.

As Hugh came near the castle he saw the giant and his wife standing on the steps

'My father,' said she, 'banished from his kingdom a wicked giant. The giant's brother in revenge seized me and kept me imprisoned here.'

'But,' said Hugh, 'how did the giant take you from your father's home? Are there not guards and attendants there?'

'Yes,' said Maca, 'but the giant found out that I liked to walk alone in a lovely wood which is near the palace. One spring day as I was gathering violets, he came and bore me away so quickly that I could not even call for help.'

'Where is your father's castle?' Hugh asked.

'It is near the western coast and is so far away that I fear I shall never see my home again.'

Hugh led the princess down to the water's edge. There stood the seagull. Hugh touched it with the feather. As he did it grew so large that he and Maca were able to mount on its back. It flew westwards over lakes and plains, over hills and valleys, till it reached a beautiful glen in the midst of the blue hills of Donegal.

There stood the castle before them, its windows shining like gold in the rays of the setting sun.

They dismounted from the seagull and the bird flew swiftly away.

No words can describe the joy of the king and queen when they saw their daughter again. Maca told her parents all about her escape from the giant's castle and of Hugh's kindness and courage.

'You are a brave man,' said the king, 'and I should like to make you one of the chieftains of the kingdom.'

'That would be a great honour,' said Hugh, 'and

nothing would please me better except something which is almost too good to ask for.'

'I know what that is,' said the queen. 'It is our daughter's hand in marriage.'

Hugh looked at Maca.

She placed her hand in his, saying, 'As I have already given you my heart, you may now take my hand.'

The happy pair were married amid scenes of great rejoicing and lived happily ever after.

Jack and his Animals

Years and years ago there lived in that part of Ireland which is now County Tyrone a man named Lorcan with Brid his wife and Jack their only child, a boy in his teens.

They had been happy and fairly comfortable till the father lost his health. He had worked very hard to provide a good home for his wife and child but his health broke down under the strain of the hard labour.

Jack was a kind, loving boy. As he grew older he felt he should find some means of helping to make life easier and happier for his parents.

He was very fond of animals and had wonderful power in training them and winning their affection.

'Mother,' he said one day, 'I have thought of a plan to make life easier and more comfortable for you and my father. We have four animals here, the ass, the dog, the cat and the goat.'

'Well, Jack Alanna, what do you mean to do?'

'You know, Mother, I have trained the animals to play tricks and I have thought that perhaps I could earn money by amusing the people who would see them performing.'

'Certainly, Jack, you have done extraordinary work in

teaching the beasts. Not only do they perform wonderfully but they also enjoy the play.'

'Well, Mother, I will start on my travels at once and I promise you I will return home as soon as possible.'

Jack made all things ready and set off. He took his fife with him.

The parents stood side by side at the window of the room where the poor invalid passed his days. They waved a loving farewell to their good son.

He, with the four animals, travelled on till they reached a field near a small town.

Jack placed the animals in a row, took out his fife and began to play. Immediately the four responded to the music. The ass began to bray, the dog to bark, the cat to mew and the goat to bleat.

In a little while most of the people in the neighbourhood assembled in the field to listen to the 'band'.

After a short time Jack stopped playing. Immediately the animals followed his example.

One old lady, a lover of animals who had been brought out to witness the performance, gave orders to have a good meal prepared at her house for Jack and his animals. Both man and beasts thoroughly enjoyed the food. She also gave Jack a good sum of money.

Jack wished to derive as much profit as possible from the long day.

He gathered his band together and started off to go to another town. When they reached it he arranged the animals in order on a patch of waste ground.

The music started. In a short time it seemed as if all the people of the town were gathered together to hear and see the strange band. The animals themselves seemed to enjoy the game.

Among the crowd was a rich man named Feilim, with Finola his wife and Maeve their seven-year-old daughter.

'Father, where are the man and the animals going now?' Maeve asked.

Jack himself answered the question. 'We will travel a bit farther and reach a wood. We can sleep under the trees.'

'Oh!' said Feilim, 'rain might come on and you would have no shelter.'

'There is a big empty shed near the back of our house,' said Finola. 'The animals could sleep there. You yourself can find a bed in the house.'

Both Jack and his animals slept comfortably that night. They started off early next morning after having a good breakfast.

Feilim with his wife and daughter stood at the gate of the house to say goodbye. Maeve had been given a purse of money to put into Jack's hand. He was delighted to think of the joy the money would bring to his parents.

He travelled on till he came to a splendid mansion surrounded by trees. It was the home of a wealthy chieftain named Angus, Anna his wife, and their daughter, Eva.

They had been for years a very happy family but were now a sad one.

Eva was a beautiful girl and was as good as she was beautiful.

A marriage had been arranged between her and a fine young chieftain named Oscar.

Immediately the four responded to the music

All preparations had been made when a sad occurrence put an end to the joyful anticipation.

One lovely spring day Eva and two of her companions, Brid and Siobhan, went for a walk along a winding road known as The Witch's Lane.

It was so called because a wicked witch had her home there among the bushes and brambles.

The witch was feared by the people of the neighbourhood.

It was said she put cruel spells on anyone who dared to go near her dwelling place.

When the three girls came towards it Siobhan and Brid turned back but Eva went on.

'I am not afraid of the ugly old creature,' she said.

She had gone only a very short distance when the hideous old hag rushed out from among the bushes.

She had a crooked stick in her hand.

With it she struck Eva on the mouth as she said:

> 'Power of speech you'll ne'er regain
> All help and cures will be in vain
> Till strange, quaint music greets your ear
> And drives away all doubt and fear.'

Laughing and cackling the witch rushed back towards her den.

In her savage delight she forgot the deep lake near her home. She stumbled over a large stone. In vain she tried to reach the brambles. The water seemed to drag her down, down. She was never heard of more.

Her wicked power had put poor Eva under a cruel spell. She was deprived of the power of speech.

Oscar wished the marriage to take place as arranged but Eva herself would not consent to such an arrangement.

Jack happened to select for his next performance a field near Eva's house.

The day was bright and sunny. The birds were singing and the blossoms were sprouting on the trees. Scenes of beauty and renewed life appeared on all sides.

Angus, his wife, daughter and Oscar were seated at the mid-day meal when they heard the sound of extraordinary music.

Eva loved music. She rushed without ceremony from the table and hurried to the place from whence the sound had come.

The parents and Oscar followed her. All four were amazed to see Jack and his band. The sight was a fantastic and funny one.

The poor donkey was getting tired but he kept on bravely with his part so as to hold his place in the orchestra.

The dog kept on changing the key from threatening growls to barks of joy and welcome.

The cat mewed loudly but now and again softened the tone to a gentle purr.

The meg geg geg of the goat was somewhat nasal but was constant and well sustained.

The parents and Oscar listened for a moment to the 'choir' but what was their joy when they turned towards Eva and saw that she was laughing heartily.

'Oh! Father, Mother, Oscar,' she cried, 'the cruel spell is broken. The witch's prophecy has come true. Strange, quaint music has been my cure.'

All the listeners came forward with generous money gifts.

Angus asked Jack what were his plans for the future.

'I will go home now to my parents,' was his reply.

'Is your home far from here?'

'Well, it is a good distance.'

'Oh! then we must find some means of sending you back.'

'Do you remember, Father,' said Eva, 'there are wagons in the stables that would take more than twice the number of animals? And Jack himself could be sent home on one of the side-cars.'

The triumphant march home began. Jack received a tumultuous welcome from all his neighbours and friends.

With great care and good food the father regained his health and both people and animals lived happily ever after.

A Prince in Disguise

Prince Cormac was the only child of King Oriel and Queen Aoife.

The great desire of the parents' hearts was to see their son happily married. They determined to speak to him about choosing a wife.

'Cormac,' said the King, 'you must marry. Surely you will not allow the throne to descend to a stranger.'

'And,' added the Queen, 'our great possessions to pass out of the family.'

'But, Mother, I am content as I am. Where could I find a wife I would love as I love you? and where could I find one with such beautiful raven hair and sparkling eyes as yours?'

'You yourself, Cormac, have inherited your mother's beautiful eyes and hair,' said the King.

Cormac possessed many natural gifts. He was handsome and brave and had won the affection of his people by his kindness and charm.

Among his many manly qualities was his skill as an athlete. He was almost tired of receiving homage and praise for his achievements on the sports field.

'Fergal,' he said one day to his best friend, 'it is because

I am the Prince that such great tribute is paid to my athletic triumphs.'

'Nonsense,' said Fergal, 'the applause is thoroughly deserved.'

'Well, I intend to put the sincerity to the test. I want you to help me to disguise myself and I shall play as an ordinary hurler.'

'And how will you arrange all that?'

'The players will be waiting for the arrival of the Prince and when he does not appear I in my disguise will offer to fill the vacant place so that the game may be played.'

'Well, you have always enjoyed jokes and pranks. I hope this one will turn out to your satisfaction.'

The day for the contest arrived. The players on both sides were ready for the game, but where was the Prince?

'The match must proceed,' said the captain on one side.

'Yes,' agreed the other captain. 'It would be unlucky to postpone it. It must be played today for the new moon will appear tonight and our matches are timed for the first appearance of the new moon.'

At this point in the conversation Cormac, wearing a wig and cleverly disguised, came forward and spoke in a foreign language. Fergal answered in the same language.

'The game may go on as usual,' he said, 'if this player is allowed to take the vacant place.'

'By all means he will be allowed to play,' said one of the captains.

'And indeed,' said the captain of the other side, 'we are all very thankful to him for enabling us to proceed with the game.'

Opposite the ground where the match was to be played there was a beautiful castle. It had belonged to a chieftain named Niall who lived there with Maeve his wife and their daughter Etain.

Maeve had died and after some years Niall had married a widow named Sorcha who had a daughter, Grainne.

The second wife seemed at first to be very kind.

'I will be a mother to Etain, your dear child,' she said, 'and though Grainne is some years older than your daughter they will love each other like sisters.'

There is a proverb in Irish which says 'Time is a good story-teller.' It had a sad story to tell about poor Etain. Her father died.

After his death Sorcha and Grainne showed themselves in their true colours. They were very cruel to Etain. Grainne hated her.

'Mother,' she would say, 'how is it that Etain looks more beautiful in her old clothes than I do in all my grandeur?'

'Never mind, my dear. We will keep her out of the way and no one will know how beautiful she is.'

Poor Etain had a very unhappy life.

Sorcha and Grainne were among the spectators at the great match. From a small hillock on the side of the field they watched the play.

Etain longed to see the game. She managed to steal out of the house and got a place among the crowd. Like all the onlookers her eyes were fixed in admiration on one of the players who outshone all the others. His movements were swift and accurate and it might be said that the game centred round him.

Suddenly a ball whizzed towards him. There was a wail from the crowd as it struck him. He fell to the ground just near the place where Etain stood.

In her excitement she rushed towards him and raised his head. As she did so the fair wig fell away and the black, curling hair was revealed.

'Prince Cormac, Prince Cormac,' came the shout from the crowd.

For a moment Cormac opened his eyes and gazed at the fair face bending over him. Then he became unconscious.

'Let the Prince be brought to my house,' said Sorcha, 'and send at once for medical aid.'

To the joy of all concerned the doctor said the injury was not serious. Rest and quiet were all that was necessary for complete recovery.

Sorcha and Grainne were delighted to have the Prince for their guest.

'Dress in your finest clothes, my daughter, and sing your sweetest songs,' said Sorcha. 'Do your best to charm and entertain the Prince.'

Now Cormac was particularly musical. The harsh, out-of-tune singing that he was forced to listen to nearly drove him mad. News of the accident had, of course, been sent to the palace.

The King was absent from home when the message arrived but the Queen set out at once to go to her son.

There was much delay on the journey. A rain storm had come on and travelling was very difficult. Shortly before the end of the journey the weather changed and the sun shone brightly.

As the carriages approached the castle, beautiful singing was heard from inside the orchard.

'Stop the carriages for a while,' ordered the Queen.

The singing ceased but out from the orchard came a lovely girl. Her fair hair had come loose and had fallen on her shoulders like a golden fleece.

The Queen could not restrain her admiration.

'Fair maiden, what is your name?' she asked.

'Etain is my name, your Majesty.'

Just then a huge, tall man came running towards Etain.

'Hurry, hurry, *asthore*,' he said. 'Your step-mother is calling and you know the sort of temper she has.'

When Queen Aoife reached the castle Sorcha and Grainne went down on their knees to welcome her.

'I am thankful,' said the Queen, 'for the hospitality and kindness you have shown to the Prince, my son.'

'Oh, your Majesty, it has been a privilege and an honour to have him with us.'

The Prince was delighted to see his mother.

After some time the Queen said:

'As we were passing the orchard I heard most beautiful singing.'

'It must have been Grainne, my daughter, your Majesty heard,' said Sorcha. 'She has a wonderful voice.'

'Yes, Mother,' said Cormac with a slight wink, 'she has indeed quite a wonderful voice.'

'When we reached the entrance to the orchard a lovely girl came out. I thought perhaps she was the singer.'

'Oh! Not at all,' said Grainne, 'she was merely one of the servants.'

'Though she was poorly dressed,' said the Queen, 'she

looked very beautiful with the sunshine gleaming on her golden hair.'

'Mother,' exclaimed Cormac, 'I have seen a girl like that in my dreams.'

'Your Majesty,' said Sorcha, 'the Prince has been delirious nearly all the time since the accident. Nothing soothes him but a drink which I prepare for him.'

Cormac looked at the Queen and said, 'Is it not strange, Mother, that I feel bright and strong till I take the drink. After having it I become dull and listless.'

The Queen turned to Sorcha, saying: 'Thank you for your hospitality and kindness, which I hope to repay. I shall have arrangements made to take the Prince home as soon as possible.'

The Queen departed but soon returned to take Cormac home.

Sorcha and Grainne were determined that neither Cormac nor the Queen would see Etain. They had the girl locked in a room at the top of the house. No one was allowed to go near her.

There was only one person in the household who dared to befriend Etain. This was poor, simple Conn, who did most of the slavish work round the kitchens. He was a huge, strong fellow, but for all his size and strength he was very gentle and kind. All the animals round the house loved and trusted him.

Conn had a great affection for Etain. She told him all her troubles.

Very shortly before the departure of the Queen and Cormac, Conn rushed upstairs to the locked room.

'Are you there, my girl?' he asked through the keyhole.

'Yes, Conn,' came the reply.

Conn hurled his great body against the door. The lock broke and he was soon in the room.

'Come quietly, *asthore*. They are getting ready for the journey. We will slip out by the back door.'

Etain followed Conn. Before long they were out on the road.

The moon was shining brightly.

'Now,' said Conn, 'when we come to the orchard gate stand still. Leave the rest to me.'

Queen Aoife, Cormac and their retinue left the castle to the great disappointment of Sorcha and her daughter.

When the carriages were approaching the orchard, Conn rushed in front of them waving his hands.

'Stop, stop,' he said. 'Look towards the orchard gate.'

All eyes turned to where Etain stood in the moonlight. Her beautiful hair stirred lightly in the faint breeze.

'Mother,' exclaimed Cormac, 'that is the face I have seen in my dreams.'

Conn came to the carriage door.

'Oh, Queen,' he said, 'take pity on a poor, tortured girl and save her from the cruelty of a heartless pair.'

'Mother,' said Cormac, 'please take the girl into the carriage.'

'Oh,' said Etain, 'I cannot go without Conn, my best friend.'

'There is room for all,' said the Queen.

Etain remained silent after she told why and how she had escaped from the castle.

Not so Conn.

'That is the face I have seen in my dreams'

'Won't there be hunger and thirst in the castle to-night?' he said, chuckling and rubbing his hands.

'You know, your Majesty,' he continued, 'Sorcha and her ugly daughter have fine appetites and like a good meal.'

'And will they not have one to-night?' asked Cormac.

Conn shook with laughter as he said:

'Hardly, your Highness. I collected all the hungry cats I could find and shut them in the pantries. How will it be when the cooks go to look for the milk, cream, beef, fish and all the good things that the cruel pair will be expecting for their evening meal?'

Not one of the company could refrain from joining in the hearty laughter.

The end of the story was that King Oriel and his Queen got their wish when their valiant son was married to beautiful Etain.

The Stolen Crown

Centuries and centuries ago there lived in a fine palace near Lough Corrib a king named Flann with Fidelma his queen. Their family consisted of four boys and a girl named Eimer.

Flann and Fidelma were loved by their subjects and everything went well within their dominions.

One by one the boys married. Eimer was now about eighteen years of age and was the only child left with her parents. They wished that she too would marry but among her many suitors the only one she would choose was a young chieftain named Shane. He was neither as rich nor as powerful as any of the others. Her choice did not please her father and the young pair could not marry without his consent.

An event now took place which greatly disturbed the peace and happiness of the household. Flann had a very wonderful crown. It had been worn by many of his ancestors. In it was a precious stone which was supposed to bring good luck to the wearer.

One night there was a great ball in the palace. Bright lights shone. Music, song and dance continued for hours. Joy and mirth prevailed. When the merriment was over the king felt tired. He hastened to his bedroom without waiting for his valet to attend him. He took off his crown and laid it on a table which was near the door. Suddenly the door was opened. An enormous arm and hand were extended towards the table. Like a flash the crown was gone. For a moment the king could not think or speak. When he recovered from the shock he called for help. Soon all in the palace were running here and there in a vain effort to find the thief.

The only one who seemed to have caught a glimpse of him was old Brid who had been standing near the entrance of the palace. She had seen him hasten by with something bright in his hand. Before she could call for help the strides of his long legs had borne him quickly out of sight.

Brid was an old woman who had been in the castle before the king was born. She loved all the family and was beloved by them. Eimer was especially the darling of her heart.

'It is useless to look through the house or grounds to find the thief,' she said. 'He is no other than the giant of the Black Mountain.'

The giant was the terror of the people for miles round. His home was in a place called the Black Mountain. It was so called because no grass ever grew on it and the surface was of a dark colour. Round it was a wide ditch, so wide that no one but the giant himself could cross from the road to the mountain. His huge legs enabled him to stride safely over. The ditch was always full of water so deep that it was said to be bottomless.

The king was much distressed by the loss of his crown. He sent out word that the finder of it would receive his daughter in marriage. Poor Eimer was not pleased with this statement. She sought out her loved Brid.

'Oh! Brid,' she asked, 'can you not do anything to help Shane to find the crown. You who are such a friend of the fairies?'

'Hush, *alanna*, don't talk of the fairies like that. My friendship with them must be kept a strict secret.'

'But Brid, what will I do if someone instead of Shane finds the crown?'

'Don't be uneasy, *asthore*. Leave everything to me.'

What Eimer had said about the fairies and Brid was true. She was a great friend of theirs. She waited till the midnight of the next day and then went alone to a little mound which was some distance from the palace. The moon was shining brightly. There in its light she saw her fairy friends enjoying the beauty of the night. They stopped dancing as she approached.

'*Failte romhat*' (Welcome), came in a chorus from them. 'What is your wish?'

Brid thanked them for their welcome and then told them about the stolen crown. One little man came out from among the others and said, 'We will help you to serve those you love for you are our faithful friend.'

'But,' said Brid,' the giant is very powerful and very wicked and it is impossible to reach his home in the Black Mountain.'

'Our power is greater than his,' said the fairy. 'Wait a moment.' He disappeared into the mound and returned carrying three things; a cloak, a pair of strange looking shoes and a sword.

'Take this cloak,' he said. 'It makes the wearer invisible.

It is called the cloak of darkness. Look.' The fairy put on the cloak and both he and it were completely lost to sight. 'Now,' he said as he removed the cloak, 'here is a pair of shoes. They are called the shoes of swiftness. Look.' He put them on and began to walk. In a moment he had covered the length of the field. 'Now look at this sword. One tip of it is enough to kill anyone. The giant knows what power is in this weapon.'

'But,' said Brid, 'I don't want to kill anyone, even the giant.'

'You need not kill him for he will understand the power of the sword and will not tempt you to use it. Now give these three things to Shane. Tell him how to use them. One word more. Return all three to me when the work is finished.'

Brid thanked the fairy and departed. Next day she told Eimer about her visit.

'Now, *a chuisle*,' she said, 'give this cloak, those shoes and this sword to Shane. The cloak will make him invisible. The shoes will enable him to take very long strides and the sword will terrify the giant so much that he will give up the crown. Fortunately the moon is at its brightest just now.'

Poor Shane had been very unhappy because he feared he would never win Eimer for his wife. Great was his delight when Eimer told him all that had happened in the fairy field. To him midnight seemed to be a long time coming. As the time drew near he took the cloak, the shoes and the sword and started off for the Black Mountain.

The giant was still abroad looking for what plunder he

could find. Suddenly Shane saw him approaching. He put on the cloak of darkness. The giant advanced. He crossed over the ditch with one step. Then he climbed to the top of the mountain and descended on the other side. Though Shane had put on the cloak of darkness when he saw the giant, he himself could see everything while wearing it. He took off the cloak and put on the shoes of swiftness. With their aid he stepped quickly across the ditch. He was standing at the foot of the mountain when the giant returned from the other side. Shane kept the sword concealed under his right arm.

'How does a pigmy like you dare to come here?' asked the giant.

'I have come to demand the return of the king's crown which you have stolen! Give it to me without delay.'

The giant burst out laughing. 'Who are you,' he said, 'that you should dare to speak to me like that? One blow from my hand would knock you lifeless.'

Shane drew the sword from the scabbard as he said: 'And one thrust from this sword would render *you* lifeless.'

The giant uttered a loud cry – 'The magic sword of sharpness,' he said. 'Oh! put up that sword and I will grant you every wish.'

'I will sheath the sword after you have given me the crown.'

'Come with me,' said the giant.

He led Shane to a small cave on the side of the mountain. Inside was the crown carefully covered from all damp and injury. Shane kept the sword in his right hand all this time. With the other he grasped the crown. While

Shane drew the sword from the scabbard

doing so he moved his right hand. The giant started and in terror moved. He feared Shane was going to kill him. In moving he missed his footing and fell down into the bottomless ditch. He was no longer a terror to the neighbourhood.

Shane hurried away. With the aid of the shoes of swiftness he reached the fairy fort before the revels were ended. There was a great welcome for him.

'Here is your valuable property,' he said. 'All three served me well. The giant will trouble us no more.'

'Did you kill him with the sword of sharpness?' asked one of the fairies.

'No. I am glad to say I did not kill him.'

'Then why do you say he will trouble us no more?' asked another fairy.

'Because he fell into the ditch and we all know that no one ever comes out of that ditch, dead or alive.'

Shane thanked the fairies and hurried away. He went to the palace early next morning before any of the family were stirring. He sought out Brid.

'Oh! you are a wonder, Brid,' he said. 'With your advice and help I have been able to bring back the crown.'

'Oh! tell me how you got it.'

Shane gave Brid a full account of his adventures with the fairies and the giant.

'Now,' said Brid, 'we must arrange things so as to give the family a great surprise. I will put the crown in the centre of the table. I myself will hide behind one of the window curtains and watch the result of my plan.'

'I will go away now, Brid,' said Shane.

'Very well, *a mhic*, but I can say with truth that it will not be long till you will return here.'

Flann, his wife and daughter came into the room together. They stood still in amazement, amazement followed by rapture.

'Oh! who has found the crown?' asked the king.

'I can answer that question,' said Brid, as she came out from her hiding place.

'Oh! Brid, Brid, tell us quickly, quickly how the crown has been found,' said the queen.

Eimer's heart was beating wildly but she remained silent.

'Well, Your Majesties, I cannot give you an account of the way it has been found. That must remain a secret but I can tell you who has recovered and brought it safely back.'

'Oh! Brid,' said the king with some impatience, 'tell us at once who brought it back.'

Eimer's heart was beating fast as Brid answered. 'It was no other than the brave champion Shane.'

'Have him brought here at once,' said the king.

The queen put her arms round Eimer. Neither of them spoke.

'Brid, make no delay,' said the king. 'Summon Shane here without delay.'

It was not long till Shane appeared.

'My noble boy,' said the king, 'how can I thank you? My gratitude and affection will now atone for my refusal to give my consent for a marriage between you and my daughter. I now declare that from among all her suitors you are the one of my choice.'

'You have been mine long before this,' said the queen as she took Shane's hand in hers.

Eimer remained silent but was very happy.

'And now, Shane,' said the king, 'will you please tell us how you recovered the crown.'

'Your Majesty, that is something I cannot do. I am under *geasa* [magical spell or injunction] not to disclose the facts connected with the finding of the crown.'

'The main point is that the crown has been found,' said the queen, 'and Shane must be allowed to keep his secret.'

There was a magnificent wedding. Shane and Eimer lived a very happy life. They had many children whose delight it was to hear their parents tell them stories of the olden time. Whether in the gardens in the sunny summer days or round the blazing fires in winter they never tired of listening to the tales of long ago.

From old Brid they heard about the giant that stole the king's crown but were never told how it was found again.

The Witch's Spell

Once upon a time, long, long ago, there lived in the South of Ireland a king named Oiliol and his queen, Sile.

One lovely summer morning word was sent out that a baby girl had been born in the palace. The news brought joy throughout the kingdom, for the royal pair were beloved by their subjects.

> Bells were rung
> Songs were sung
> And music filled the air
> The morn was bright
> All hearts were light
> And joy reigned everywhere.

'What name shall we give the child?' asked Oiliol.

'We will call her Griana,' said the Queen, 'because she came into the world with the rising sun.'

There was, however, one in the neighbourhood who did not share in the general rejoicing. This was an old hag named *Bandraoi* [witch] so called from her power in magic. She lived in a hut not far from the palace. Strange shrubs grew in her little garden. There was a large deep well at the back of the house.

Bandraoi was feared by all the people from near and far.

The reason for this was that it was believed she had the power of casting spells on those who dared to refuse her requests or to differ from her in any way.

One day when Griana was about a month old, Noinin, her nurse, carried her out into the bright sunshine.

As she was passing Bandraoi's house the witch herself appeared at the door. She had a short stick in her hand.

'Her wand!' thought Noinin as she turned back quickly towards the palace. Bandraoi hurried after her and overtook her just before she reached the gates.

'Let me hold the child for a moment,' she said.

Noinin refused this request.

The witch raised the wand and touched the lips of the sleeping child.

Then she said these words in harsh, grating tones:

> 'From this for you unlucky day
> I take the power of speech away
> Henceforth through all the years to come
> Hark! You shall be for ever dumb.'

With a harsh laugh and threatening aspect she hurried back to her home.

Next morning she did not appear.

For a couple of days she was not seen. Some children who were curious to know where she was ventured to climb into her little garden. They found her lying dead in the well. A pitcher was in her hand. Evidently she had fallen into the water while trying to fill it.

Griana grew to be a lovely girl. Her sight and hearing

were perfect, but, alas! the witch's spell had taken effect. The poor girl was dumb. Her parents tried every means to restore her power of speech. All in vain. She was very clever and learned to play the harp with great skill.

Years passed. Griana was now a grown girl. Her parents almost worshipped her.

'She is very beautiful,' the mother would say, 'but what man would care to marry a dumb girl? What will be her fate when we are gone?'

The father tried to be more hopeful.

'Well, Sile,' he would say, 'we must not worry too much about the future. After all she will inherit our great wealth and will always receive service and respect.'

One day while Griana was walking in the gardens visitors arrived at the palace.

They were Princess Blathnaid, a rich widow, and her son Caroll.

All the love of Blathnaid's heart was given to her son. She wished to see him happily married but feared it would be hard to find a wife who would be worthy of him.

'The girl he marries must be perfect in every way,' she would say.

When Griana returned from her walk she was surprised to see the visitors.

Both mother and son were struck by her beauty.

Griana went towards them smiling sweetly and showing signs of welcome. They were much surprised that she did not speak.

'You are tired, Griana, after your long walk,' said the mother. 'Go and rest awhile.'

When Griana had left Blathnaid said:

'How very beautiful your daughter is!'

'Yes,' said the father, 'but you must have noticed that she did not speak. Our poor child is dumb.'

'Yes,' said the mother, 'a cruel spell was placed on her when she was an infant and she has never been able to utter a word.'

'How was the spell laid on her?' asked Caroll.

'A wicked witch who lived near our home, by her evil magic, deprived our child of the power of speech.'

'I have always heard that what is caused by evil magic can be cured by the good fairies,' said Caroll.

'Perhaps that is so,' said Oiliol, 'but where shall we find the good fairy?'

'Our child has all her other senses in perfection and she seems to be perfectly happy.'

'Mother,' said Caroll, when they were alone together, 'what a beautiful girl Griana is. It is just a tragedy for her to be deprived of the power of speech.'

'Indeed I have been thinking how sad and unfortunate it is that she cannot speak. But for that she would have been the girl I would have most wished to be your wife. She is rich, beautiful and clever, but the fact that she is dumb would be a great impediment to a marriage with you.'

Blathnaid and Caroll remained for some time at the palace.

Though Griana could not speak it was a joy to all to have her at the balls and other festivities.

Caroll spent much time listening to her playing the harp. As the days went by he longed more and more to be with her.

They danced together, rode together and understood each other even though poor Griana could not speak.

One night there was a great ball in the palace. Griana was as happy as anyone there. She looked beautiful in her exquisite dress and costly jewels. Caroll spent much time by her side.

When all was over and Blathnaid had gone to her room she heard a knock at her door. When she opened it she found Caroll outside.

'I want to speak to you, Mother,' he said.

'Well, come in but be brief, for I am tired and long to sleep. You too must be weary for I noticed you danced very often, especially with Griana.'

'I am not at all tired and I want to tell you something of great importance.'

'Something of great importance! Well, what is it, my son?'

'I have found the girl I should like to marry.'

The mother looked somewhat startled.

'Tell me her name,' she said.

'Griana is her name.'

The mother's face grew pale.

'Griana!' she exclaimed. 'You cannot possibly marry Griana.'

'Why not?' asked Caroll.

'A girl who cannot speak! Picture your life, married to a dumb creature.'

'Well, Mother, she is the girl of my choice. You were anxious I should marry. I have found the girl I would choose as my wife.'

'Please leave me, Caroll. This news has overpowered me.'

'But, Mother, you wished that I would marry.'

'Marry, yes, but marry a suitable wife. Please leave me, Caroll, to think over the matter. I cannot entertain the idea of a marriage such as you speak of.'

Caroll was very much depressed by his mother's attitude. He did not see her next day. She complained of being tired and ill and did not leave her room.

The next great event that took place was a big hunt. All the friends in the neighbourhood assembled to join in it.

The weather was beautiful and all started off in great glee.

The poor fox eluded his pursuers for a long time. He was almost exhausted when he reached a mountain which was near the palace.

It was at the foot of this mountain poor Renard had his lair.

Caroll had the swiftest horse and was considerably in advance of the other hunters.

Suddenly it occurred to him how cruel it was to further pursue the poor animal.

He called off the hounds. Like a flash Renard reached his home.

The other members of the hunt were indignant with Caroll.

'You have spoiled the sport,' said one.

'Hearts can be too soft,' said another.

Well, everything in this world passes and so did the disappointment of the hunters.

As the day wore on Caroll felt sad and depressed.

His mother had not left her room since he had told her he wished to marry Griana.

He loved his mother very much and would be sorry to displease her.

When night came on and all was quiet in the palace he went out in the moonlight. He cared not what way he took. After walking for some time he found himself at the foot of the mountain where the fox had his lair. Near it was a fairy fort.

As he approached it he saw a tiny man sitting under a rowan tree. When he came nearer the tree the little man stood up and said:

'You did a kind deed today.'

'What kind deed do you speak of?' asked Caroll.

'You spared the life of the fox which lives close to our home.'

'Yes, he disappeared into the mountain.'

'This fort is the fairies' home and the mountain is under our protection. I see you are in trouble. Tell me the cause of your sorrow.'

Caroll told the fairy that he wished to marry Griana.

'And why do you not do so?' he asked.

'My mother does not wish me to marry her.'

'For what reason?'

'Because the Princess cannot speak.'

'What caused her to be dumb?'

'When she was very young a wicked witch touched her lips with a hazel rod. She has never been able to utter a word.'

'Now,' said the fairy, 'what was caused by the hazel wand can be cured by the hazel tree.'

'But where shall I find that tree?'

'Listen carefully and I shall tell you. The hazel wood is far from here. I warn you the journey will cause you much fatigue.'

'I would endure much to restore speech to the Princess.'

'Good. Now follow my instructions. Take the long road at the back of the mountain. A river runs by the side of the road. You must travel along that road till you come to the hazel wood.'

'Is it a long distance from here to the wood?'

'Yes, but if you start early in the morning and follow my instructions you will be safely home the day after tomorrow.

'Now listen to further instructions. You will be hungry, thirsty and sleepy.'

'Yes, how shall I procure food, drink and rest?'

'To that question I will answer – Do you rely on me to provide everything necessary for the journey?'

'Yes.'

'Very well. Take this table napkin. When you feel hungry spread it on the grass and watch the result.

'Take this goblet and fill it from a well you will see under an ash tree on the roadside.

'Take this stick. When you feel sleepy turn it upside down.

'Ask me no more questions about food, drink or rest.

'When you reach the hazel wood pluck the largest nut on the tallest branch.'

'But how shall I return home?'

'You will find a boat moored in the river by the side of the road on which you have travelled.

'Loosen the moorings. A fairy wind will waft you back in a short time.

'When you return seek out the Princess. Touch her lips with the nut. Watch the happy effect. Ask me no more questions. Follow closely my directions and all will be well. *Slán leat.*'

The fairy vanished.

Caroll returned to the house. All was still and silent there. At dawn he started on his journey. The country was beautiful under the rays of the rising sun. He walked briskly, full of hope that all would be well. He had gone a considerable number of miles when he began to feel hungry. Remembering the fairy's instructions he spread the napkin on a green patch under a tree.

To his surprise, indeed to his amazement, he saw a substantial meal before him. He ate heartily. As he had finished the napkin rose into the air. He gazed at it till it had vanished in the clouds. He travelled on for a considerable distance. The day was now warm. He felt thirsty. He watched by the side of the river for the well. When he found it he had a delightful drink of the clear, cool water.

The goblet, like the table napkin, vanished from his sight.

Feeling refreshed he continued his journey.

The sun was now setting. A light breeze stirred the leaves on the trees. Twilight had come. He felt weary and somewhat footsore. Just before darkness fell he turned the stick. There, sheltered by a large spreading tree appeared a bed with pillows and bed clothes all complete.

He lay down and was soon in a sound dreamless sleep.

In the morning he was wakened by the cry of a bird which soared towards the sky.

As he rose from the bed it disappeared as the napkin and goblet had done.

He now saw before him the wood of which the fairy had spoken.

He entered it and found the tallest tree.

He sought out the largest nut and plucked it.

With light heart he hurried towards the river.

There was the boat of which the fairy had spoken.

He loosened the moorings. A breeze arose and he was wafted back to the mountain side.

Wonder followed by fear and anxiety were felt by all in the palace when Caroll did not appear for nearly two days.

Blathnaid was very much concerned by his absence.

'Where can he be?' she cried. 'What has befallen him? My dear son! Oh! that I had not spoken so harshly to him.'

Oiliol and Sile were equally anxious but perhaps the one who grieved most of all was poor Griana.

When Caroll left the boat it disappeared as did all the other property of the fairies.

He hurried towards the palace. As he approached it he saw Griana sitting in the garden. Her back was towards him. He stole quietly to the seat, leaned over and touched her lips with the nut.

She started up, held out her hands towards him and called out 'Caroll!'

He sought out the largest nut and plucked it

'Oh! I can speak. How has this all happened?'

'Wait a while and I will tell you all. Come now to your parents and my mother till they share in our joy.'

Oiliol, Sile and Blathnaid were sitting in one of the magnificent rooms in the palace. Neither wealth nor beauty had any charm for them.

'Oh! where is my son?' were the words uttered by Blathnaid just as the young pair reached the door.

'Here,' came the answer from Griana, 'he has come back and has brought the power of speech to me.'

Astonishment and delight held all three silent.

Blathnaid was the first to recover from the wonderful surprise.

'Oh! how has this happened?' she asked.

Before an answer could be given Sile clasped Griana in her arms and said: 'Tell us, *asthore*, how this miracle has taken place.'

'It has been brought about, Mother, by the bravery and devotion of Caroll.'

'Tell us, please, Caroll,' said Oiliol, 'what magic power you possess, for nothing but magic could have broken the witch's power and given speech to our loved child.'

Caroll then gave a full account of this meeting with the fairy and his visit to the hazel wood.

'I have always heard,' said Sile, 'that the fairies remember kind and unkind actions and that they reward or punish those who do them. We will all in future regard with care the fairy fort.'

When the excitement was over and all the party had settled down for a quiet chat Blathnaid said:

'We have remained long in your hospitable company. We really must now return home.'

'I must ask leave,' said Caroll, 'to return here soon and take Griana to another home.'

'What does this mean?' asked Oiliol.

'It means,' said Caroll, 'that Griana and I are going to get married.'

'And live happily ever after,' said Griana as she took her harp and sang:

> 'Sing a song of glee
> Sorrow has departed
> Happy now are we
> Joyous and lighthearted
> Caroll brave and strong
> With love and strength did sever
> Power which held me long
> Now I'm his for ever.'

Well! there was a great wedding and Caroll and Griana lived happily ever after.

The Spoiled Child

Once upon a time there lived near the beautiful Erne lakes a rich man named Diarmuid and his wife Mella. They had an only child named Aisling. She was very beautiful and was the delight and pride of her parents' hearts. They granted her every wish. She was brought up to think only of herself.

'The darling child must have everything she wishes for,' the mother would say.

'Yes,' agreed the father, 'she is our only child and must be spared all trouble and sorrow. It is good to think we are rich enough to give her everything she desires.' Indeed, it will be difficult later on to get a husband who will be deserving of her.'

'She must marry a rich and handsome man,' said the mother, 'and one who will never refuse her slightest request.'

There was only one person in the castle who had any influence on Aisling. This was Ina, her mother's sister. She saw that the child was being thoroughly spoiled. She understood her character and knew that by nature she was truthful and affectionate but was being ruined by flattery and indulgence.

'Aisling,' said Ina one day, 'try to remember there are other people in the world as well as you.'

'I know,' said Aisling, 'but naturally I matter most to myself.'

'But really, Aisling, you should be more kind and gentle than you are. I found poor Lelia crying this morning, because you had been so cross with her.'

'Well, she was stupid to leave out my blue dress when I wanted the red one.'

'She has served you well since you were a baby and you should be grateful to her instead of treating her so badly. Poor Conn, too. I heard you scolding him because he delayed in bringing round your horse.'

'You, Ina, are always finding fault with me and yet I like talking to you. I suppose one gets tired of sweet things and would like a little acid now and again.'

'Oh,' laughed Ina, 'am I as sour as that?'

Turning to the window she said: 'I see Ronan on his horse waiting to go out to ride with you.'

'He can wait,' said Aisling, going out of the room.

Ronan was the son of another rich man who lived at a short distance from Aisling's home. He, like her, was an only child. They had played together from the time they were very young. Though Ronan was the elder it was Aisling who always had the choice of the games.

Years passed. Aisling as a grown girl was as beautiful as she had been as a child.

Ronan was a fine, handsome youth, but his life was a lonely one. Both his parents had died while he was still young. He loved Aisling and would have liked to make her his wife. She, however, preferred to remain the spoiled pet of her parents.

One day he and Ina were talking together.

'You are lonely here, Ronan,' said Ina. 'I would advise you to travel and see the great world.'

'I think you are right, Ina. I can never win Aisling for my wife and as you say I am lonely here.'

'Well, Ronan, you will send me messages from time to time and I shall try to keep in touch with you. Don't stay away too long. Remember Ireland is your home.'

'Oh, I will surely return. I will arrange with Connel, my trusty servant, to look after the land.'

'And I,' said Ina, 'will see that the house is kept in order.'

Soon after this Ronan went away. He did not say goodbye to anyone.

On the morning after his departure Aisling thought she would like a ride.

'Ina,' said she, 'will you send word to Ronan to come with his horse.'

'Ronan will not come,' said Ina.

'Will not come! Why pray?'

'He has gone abroad.'

Aisling was now pale and trembling. 'Why was I not told of his departure?'

'Would you have cared?' asked Ina, somewhat bitterly.

Aisling went quickly from the room. That evening Ina found her in the little garden of Ronan's house. She was sobbing bitterly.

Ina was determined to cure Aisling of her selfishness.

She knew she would never have true friends or real happiness until she learned to think more of others and less of herself.

With these thoughts in her mind she went to talk with a friend whom she had known from childhood. This friend was an old woman named Lasar. Lasar was a *bean feasa* [woman of knowledge]. She was descended from a druidical family and had magical powers. These she practised for only a very few. Ina was among these favoured ones.

Her cottage was situated under a spreading tree in a little lane not far from the castle. When Ina entered she found Lasar sitting on a low seat and gazing into the fire. She beckoned to Ina to sit on a stool opposite her.

'*Failte* [welcome],' said she, 'I knew you were coming.'

'How did you know?'

'I saw there in the fire the picture of a dark woman.'

Ina, like Aisling, had beautiful dark hair.

'Well, what can I do for you?'

'Lasar, I want you to use your magic power to soften Aisling's heart and make her kind and thoughtful.'

'Magic power will help, but she must first encounter danger and suffering and bring relief where she finds them.'

'How can she be brought to see anything unpleasant or dangerous? Her parents have spared her trouble and worry all her life.'

'Are her parents at home at present?'

'No, they have gone to visit friends and will not return for some time.'

'Why did Aisling not go with them?'

'They would have liked her to go but when she said she would prefer to stay at home she, of course, was allowed to remain.'

Lasar rose and went to a cupboard in the wall. She took out what looked like a tin bracelet.

'Give this to Aisling and tell her to wear it and to follow the directions which you will give her.'

'But what directions am I to give her?'

'She is to go out three mornings in succession and relieve any pain or trouble which she will see on her way. If she refuses to help she will feel the bracelet pressing into her flesh. If she helps the bracelet will turn into the colour signified by the kind action she performs.'

'I know Aisling will be delighted to wear the bracelet. She has always been anxious to get something from your magic store.'

Aisling gladly took the bracelet.

In the morning she went out and walked towards the nearby village. Just before she reached it she saw a woman sitting in an armchair near a little house. Suddenly the woman began to scream. Then Aisling noticed that the thatched roof of the house was on fire.

'I cannot move,' said the woman, 'and there is a baby in a cradle inside the house and no one else there.'

Aisling hesitated. Then she felt a slight pressure of the bracelet on her arm. She rushed into the house and carried out the cradle. At once the bracelet turned to gold.

Some people from the village then arrived and extinguished the fire. Later on the parents of the baby came on the scene. They had been working in the fields.

'Oh!' said the mother, 'our little house is destroyed.'

'Don't fret,' said Aisling kindly, 'I will send work-men tomorrow to repair it or build a new one.'

Amidst the thanks and blessings of the people she returned home.

'Good girl,' said Ina when she heard all that had happened.

'Oh, Ina,' said Aisling, 'I was very sorry for the poor people. Just think how we would feel if our house were burned, and look, Ina, at the wonderful change that has come on the bracelet. It has turned to gold.'

Ina remembered Lasar's words.

Next morning Aisling went out again. This time she walked by the sea. The shore was deserted except that at some distance an old man was sitting on the rocks.

All at once he began to yell and wave his arms. Aisling hurried towards him.

'Look,' he said, pointing out to sea, 'my little grand-son is drowning. I cannot reach him. I cannot swim.'

The child had gone to bathe and had gone out of his depth.

Aisling felt the faintest tightening of the bracelet. She was an expert swimmer. She plunged into the sea and brought the child safely to land.

Immediately beautiful sapphires appeared in the bracelet.

The old man clasped the child in his arms and knelt down to bless and thank the girl who had saved him.

Ina was again delighted when she saw the sapphires. She remembered the fire was the colour of gold and the sapphires the blue of the sea.

The third morning Aisling went to walk in a wood near the house. Some men were cutting wood there. Each had an axe. One man missed his aim and struck his leg. Blood gushed forth from it. Aisling hated the sight of blood. She felt pressure from the bracelet. Tearing strips from her dress she bandaged the wound to prevent further bleeding. She then brought the man into the house so that the leg would get more treatment.

When she looked at the bracelet she saw it was studded with rubies. Aisling was now much gentler.

'The girl grows more beautiful every day,' said the mother. 'I wish she would choose a husband.'

'Yes,' replied the father, 'many suitors have come to seek her hand but her answer is "No" to each one.'

One day Ina said to Aisling, 'Aisling, you should marry.'

'There is only one man I will marry, Ina, and that is Ronan.'

Ina made no delay in sending word to Ronan to come home.

Just then a new suitor arrived at the castle. He was a prince and in time would be a king. His wealth was far in excess of any of the others who had come to ask Aisling's hand in marriage.

Diarmuid and Mella were very anxious that Aisling would marry him.

'You won't refuse to marry a prince,' said Mella. 'Why, child, you would one day be a queen.'

'You will be an ungrateful girl if you refuse to do as we wish,' said Diarmuid, 'after all the love and care we have bestowed on you. It is a shame to be so headstrong and disobedient. If you follow your own course you will all your life regret that you did not take the advice of the parents who brought you up with such wisdom and care.'

Poor Aisling was very unhappy.

One lovely spring day she was standing at the gate of the castle. Her heart was sad but as she listened to the trill of a blackbird in a tree above her a still more joyous sound reached her ears.

'Aisling.' And there was Ronan looking braver and handsomer than ever.

The welcome that she and Ina had for Ronan was not shared by Diarmuid and Mella. They refused to give their consent to a marriage with him and continued to urge Aisling to marry the prince.

As usual she went to Ina for counsel and sympathy.

'Oh, Ina, what shall I do?' she said. 'If I marry without my parents' consent they will treat me as a stranger and make me miserable for the rest of my life.'

'Courage, Aisling, all is not lost. I will go and see my friend Lasar.'

That night Lasar was about to prepare for bed when Ina knocked at the door.

The old woman listened carefully to all that Ina had to tell her.

'You say the girl has become very sweet and gentle.'

'Yes, she is now the kindest and most loving creature you could meet.'

'Ah!' said Lasar, ' "suffering keeps a hard school but those who have come through it have been wisely taught." Well, we will make everything right for the girl.'

From her cupboard she took out a large pin.

'This is the *biorán suain* [pin of sleep]. When Aisling is sound asleep put this pin in her hair. She will look as if she were dead and will remain so till the pin is removed.'

'But when will it be removed?' asked Ina.

'Wait and I will tell you all. When the parents see that there is no sign that Aisling will awaken they will be bowed down with sorrow and remorse. They will wish they had given their consent to a marriage with Ronan, thinking that might have saved her from what they believe is death. Then you, Ina, ask that Ronan may be allowed to see her. You must be kneeling at the head of the bed when he enters. Quickly withdraw the pin and all will be well. Bring the pin back to me as quickly as possible.'

Next night Aisling felt tired and sad. For some days she had been ailing. She went to bed early.

Ina waited till she was sound asleep. She slipped into the room where Aisling lay and placed the *biorán suain* in her hair.

Next morning there was consternation among the inmates of the castle. Ina alone understood what had happened. As the hours passed and Aisling showed no sign of life the distracted parents gave up hope that their child would ever waken from what they now believed was the sleep of death.

'Oh, why did we break her heart?' wailed the mother.

'She would be alive today,' said the father, 'if we had given our consent to a marriage with Ronan. Oh! if only she were alive again how happy I would be to see that marriage.'

Ina was listening attentively to all this.

The door opened to admit Ronan

'Mella,' she said, 'will you allow poor Ronan to come in and look on Aisling? You know he has suffered too.'

'Yes, let him be sent for. I am sure our poor child would like him to come.'

In a short time, Diarmuid, Mella and Ronan came to the door of Aisling's room. Ina was kneeling at the head of the bed. As the door opened to admit Ronan Ina removed the *biorán suain* from Aisling's hair.

She sat up, stretched her arms towards Ronan, and exclaimed:

'Oh! Ronan, I had an awful dream. I dreamt I was dead and just before I wakened I saw your arms extended to bring me back to life.'

Everything ended well and happily and the prince went back to his own country to find another wife.

The Fairies' Revenge

'Oh don't step inside that fairy ring, Nuala.'

'Nonsense, Conn. The fairies do not come out until midnight and they will never know I have been inside the ring.'

'I tell you, Nuala, they know everything.'

'Well, I am sure they will not see any trace of my footsteps on the soft grass. Look at those lovely white violets. I will pull a bunch of them. The "good people" would not grudge them to me.'

'Oh, Nuala, there are just as beautiful flowers growing at the other end of the field.'

'Perhaps, but I like these and will have some.'

'You are foolish, Nuala. The fairies will have revenge for this.'

'It is you who are foolish, Conn, even though you are twelve years old. Though I am two years younger I have more sense than you.'

Conn and Nuala lived with their parents in a remote place in the West of Ireland. Near their homes there were many places where the fairies were said to have their dwellings. Every hill, mound and *lios* was said to be under their sway. The children had been constantly warned not to interfere with these places.

'These are lovely violets, Nuala,' said the mother as the children came into the house. 'Where did you gather them?'

Nuala hesitated.

'Where did you gather them? Tell me,' said her father.

'At the *Fainne Si* [the fairy ring],' stammered Nuala.

'How often have you been told not to take anything from the fairy ring? Indeed, I hope no harm will come to us for this.'

Nuala loved flowers. She put the violets in a cup of water and placed the cup beside her bed.

When she went to her room that night to undress she saw that all the violets had disappeared. The cup was quite empty.

Conn was almost asleep when he heard screams from Nuala's room. He and the parents ran to see what was the matter. They found Nuala torn and bleeding. When they looked at the bed they saw that it was full of sharp thorns. The mother lifted Nuala out. The thorns immediately disappeared. Nuala lay down again. The thorns returned.

'This is the fairies' revenge,' said the mother, 'Nuala can never sleep in a bed again.'

'Let her get into mine,' said Conn.

'I fear that will not be any better,' said the father.

Nuala got into Conn's bed, but what the father said was true. The thorns were there as long as she was in the bed, but when she left it they at once disappeared.

'Oh,' said the mother, 'until the fairies' spell is broken she can never sleep in a bed again.'

There was great trouble in the house that night. Poor Nuala had to sleep on a blanket near the fire.

While the family were at breakfast next morning Sorcha, a neighbouring woman, came in.

'I came to ask for a few eggs,' she said, 'my own hens are not laying.'

'Oh! Sorcha, we are in great trouble,' said the mother.

'What is it?' said Sorcha.

When she heard what had happened she shook her head and said:

'This is a bad case. It is very hard to get free from the spell of the fairies. The only thing you can do is to try to please them in some way.'

'Do you know any way in which we could please them?' asked the father.

'Well, I believe they love music. If anyone could play for them while they are dancing they would grant any request.'

'There is no musician anywhere about here,' said the mother.

'No,' said Sorcha. 'It is a pity you, yourself, Sive, never learned music. You have a lovely singing voice. And where is there a whistler like Conn? Well, I must be going now. Thanks, Sive, for the eggs. I am sorry for Nuala, but we all know it is dangerous to interfere with the fairies.'

Conn had been listening attentively to all that was said.

'Mother, isn't it a pity that there is no one here that could play music for the fairies? I wish I could have learned to play some instrument,' he said.

'What about whistling for them, Conn,' asked the mother, laughing.

Conn could whistle any tune he heard. His whistling was so clear and sweet that the blackbirds, thrushes and other birds answered his notes. He laughed when his mother said he could whistle for the fairies but decided he would try. He waited till all the family were asleep that night. He then stole quietly out and went to the fairy ring.

The night was dark but round the ring were little glittering lights shining like stars from the flowers in the grassy ring.

One fairy was playing on a little instrument like a flute. Conn hid behind a tree. He listened for some time to the music in order to learn the air of the tune. The fairies danced round merrily.

After a time the little musician laid down his flute as if he were tired. Conn saw that the dancers were disappointed. They called out:

'We want to continue our dance.'

Conn from behind the tree began to whistle the dance tune. The fairies seemed delighted.

One of them called out:

'Who is the mortal that knows our fairy music?'

Conn, still whistling, came from behind the tree. The fairies danced and danced while he continued to whistle. At last they ceased and the Queen addressing Conn said:

'As a reward for your music we will grant any request you ask.'

'Oh,' said Conn, 'I want my sister to be released from a spell.'

'Spells are placed on those only who interfere with our dwellings,' said the Queen.

'I know that,' said Conn. 'My sister took some flowers from the ring yesterday.'

'Yes,' said the Queen, 'and by our power the flowers turned into thorns. She pulled the white violets which are our special possession. We will not allow any mortal to take anything from the ring without inflicting punishment on the human who does such an act.'

'Is there any way in which the spell can be removed?' asked Conn.

'There is and you have pleased us so much by whistling our fairy tune we will tell you how it can be done. However, it will be a hard task.'

'I will do anything to help my sister.'

'Very well. Take this basket.'

She gave him a beautiful little basket made of reeds and lined with soft green moss.

'Do not allow any mortal eye to rest on it. When you have finished your work, place it among the tall reeds on the lake side where no one will see it. We will take it away in the darkness of the night. To brighten your way take one of these lights. Put it in the basket when you are returning it.

'Now go to the end of the field and take the winding road that leads to the black mountain.'

'Is that the mountain where the black witch has her home?'

'Yes, the witch is very wicked but we have power to protect you from harm. She sleeps from midnight till dawn. Be sure you get your work done before she awakes.

'Here is what you have to do. Climb the mountain on the side that faces you as you approach it. There is a lake at the top. Round it is a row of small trees and creeping round these you will see the *dreimire gorm* [night shade, bitter sweet]. Gather as many of the leaves as you can into the basket. Hurry home and put the leaves in your sister's bed and place the bed clothes over them. The leaves will disappear. The spell will be broken and your sister's sleep will be sweet and peaceful.

'You must act quickly for if the witch hears you she will make a hole in the mountain and the water will rush down and form a cataract so that you cannot descend from that side.'

'What about the other side?' asked Conn.

'The other side is very steep and as slippery as ice, but near the top there is a large flat stone. Rub your bare feet on that stone and you will be able to get safely down.

'One thing more. You must not tell any mortal about this. Keep it all as a strict secret. *Slán leat*. Good luck.'

Conn followed all the fairy's directions.

Just as he had nearly finished gathering the leaves the day began to break.

He heard a harsh grating voice and the sound of rushing water. He hastened to the far side of the mountain. He had barely reached the stone when he saw the witch following him. She would have caught him only she stumbled and fell over a bush. Conn quickly rubbed his feet on the big stone and began to descend the mountain.

Conn looked back and saw the witch prancing with rage

As he reached the foot he heard the voice of the witch close behind him. He ran as quickly as he could but she was gaining on him. Just as she was about to catch hold of his coat he reached a stream. Witches cannot cross running water. Conn jumped across. He looked back to see her dancing and prancing with rage on the other side.

He reached home while the family were still in bed. Nuala was asleep in the blanket. Conn slipped into her room and placed the leaves in her bed and covered them with the bed clothes. Then he hurried off and put the basket back among the reeds.

When he came home breakfast was ready.

'You got up very early this morning,' said the mother.

The father who knew Conn was fond of work said:

'I am sure the lad was doing something useful.'

Conn said nothing. He thought how happy all of them would be when they knew that the cruel spell was broken. That night at bed time he said to Nuala:

'You ought to try if the thorns are still in your bed.'

'Indeed,' said the father, 'they will surely be there for how can we break the cruel spell?'

'My poor back is sore from lying on the blanket, but I know the thorns are still there,' said Nuala.

'Well,' said Conn, 'just try if they are gone.'

'Have sense,' said the mother, 'and don't bother the poor child.'

'Well, just to please me, Nuala,' urged Conn, 'lie down in the bed for a moment.'

'All right, Conn, just to please you.'

She turned down the bed clothes and lay down. There

were no thorns there. The bed was soft and comfortable and through the room there was a fragrant perfume of flowers.

'How did all this happen?' asked the father.

'Who broke the spell?' asked the mother.

Conn smiled. 'That is my secret,' he said.

'If it is a secret, my boy,' said the father, 'keep it to yourself no matter what may happen.'

And Conn kept his secret forever.

The Magic Girdle

'Ours is a miserable life,' said Cuthbert.

'Yes, indeed,' answered his brother Conleth.

'We have not enough food or clothes or any comfort.'

The speakers were the sons of Brid, a poor widow. She and Colman, her youngest son, had gone out to get sticks to keep the fire going.

They had just returned when they heard a knock at the door. When Colman opened it in came a strange looking little man. He had a long beard, bright twinkling eyes and a merry face.

'Come near the fire,' said Brid, 'the night is very cold.'

'Thank you,' said the stranger as he stretched out his hands towards the heat.

'When I saw the light,' said he, 'I came in to rest a while. Now that I am here I will tell you a story if you would like to hear one.'

'Yes, yes,' came in a chorus from all four.

'Well now, I will tell you a strange story and if you listen carefully you might hear something that would help you to become rich.'

'Oh! Tell it at once,' said Cuthbert.

'Yes,' said Conleth, 'I wish I could become rich.'

'Wishing won't bring riches or any other pleasant thing we desire, but here is my story.

'Towards the sea some miles distant from here there is a fairy mountain. The road that leads to it is also fairy ground. The mountain is not very high but it is hard to reach the summit.'

'Why is it hard to climb the mountain if it is not high?' asked Cuthbert.

'Because for every three steps you go up you fall back two.

'Some distance from the mountain there is a big house. In it there lives a rich man named Brendan with Niav, his wife and their daughter Ita.

'The garden at the back of the house is said to be fairy ground. It is understood that no one would touch a flower or shrub between the hours of sunset and dawn.

'Ita's bedroom looks out on the garden.

'One lovely spring night there were guests in the house. Ita wore some of her precious jewels. Among them was a girdle which had been in the family for generations.

'When the guests had gone she went to her own room. She stood for some time looking out the window.

'The flowers and shrubs were beautiful in the light of the moon. Silently she went downstairs and out into the garden. Forgetting all warning she pulled a branch from a hawthorn tree.

'Immediately the girdle fell at her feet and disappeared.

'Then a voice came from the tree saying these words:

"No more the girdle you will wear
Until a valiant youth shall dare
To find mid thorns the treasure there
    Upon the fairy mountain."

'For a moment the poor girl stood motionless.

'Then she fell senseless to the ground.

'When her parents missed her they thought of finding her somewhere in the house.

'Sile, her old nurse, regardless of the fairies' power went into the garden. She found her loved Ita lying on the ground, the hawthorn branch beside her.

' "Oh! the fairies!" she exclaimed.

'After a time Ita revived. She told all that had happened.

' "Alas! Mother, my precious girdle! Shall I ever recover it?"

' "Tell me, *asthore*," said Sile, "did you hear any words when the girdle was taken?"

' "Yes, and I remember them."

' "Tell us what you heard," said the father.

' "These were the words:

'No more the girdle you will wear
Until a valiant youth shall dare
To find mid thorns the treasure there
    Upon the fairy mountain.' "

' "We may yet recover the jewel," said the father. "The mountain is not far from here. It stands alone on a stretch of land at the end of the fairy lane."

' "But," said the mother, "who can be found that will climb that fairy mountain?"

'Brendan thought for a while.

'Then he said: "I will give a large portion of my wealth and my daughter in marriage to the man who will recover the girdle."

' "I agree with your decision," said Niav, "for the girdle is precious in many ways. Besides its value as a jewel it secures health and happiness for the wearer."

' "Yes," said Brendan, "and you may remember, my dear, that it has still further power. The wearer will be blessed with a good and loving husband."

'There is my story for you,' said the little man. 'Which of you will venture to climb the fairy mountain?'

'I will,' exclaimed Cuthbert and Conleth with one voice.

'You cannot go together. The eldest has the privilege of making the first attempt. If he fails the second may try. If neither succeeds there is a chance for the third.

'Now, my friends, I will continue my journey. Good-night and good luck.'

The little man went quickly out into the darkness and disappeared.

'That was a strange visitor,' said the mother. 'I think he himself belongs to the fairy world.'

Next morning for once in his life Cuthbert rose early.

'I am going to climb the fairy mountain,' he said. 'Hurry, Mother, and bake a cake that I can take with me on my journey.'

When the cake was baked Brid said: 'Now, my son,

which will you have – half the cake with my blessing, or the whole of it without my blessing?'

'Indeed, Mother, it is small enough. Give me the whole cake and let me go.'

He started off in great spirits, whistling as he went.

He had travelled some distance when he came to a small mound. A little man was sitting on the mound. There was a pair of tiny pointed shoes beside him.

He spoke these words to Cuthbert:

> 'I ask of you good friend
> Your kindly aid to lend.
>   Do not refuse.
> Good fortune you will meet
> If on my weary feet
> You place these shoes.'

'I have no time to waste on you or your shoes,' was Cuthbert's reply.

He travelled on but gave a hasty look back. The little man had disappeared.

After walking for some time Cuthbert came to a hillock on which another little man was sitting. At some distance from him there was a stick lying on the ground. It seemed as if it had fallen from his hand.

He spoke these words to Cuthbert:

> 'Oh, stranger hastening on your way
> A little moment kindly stay
>   To help me in my need.
> Restore the stick to me I pray
> Good fortune then will come your way
> And great will be your meed.'

'I have no time for you or your stick,' said Cuthbert as he hurried on. He looked back for a moment. There was no trace of the little man.

He was now getting tired, but he continued his journey. He came to a thorn tree. Standing under it was another tiny man. He seemed to be trying to extract a thorn from his hand.

He spoke to Cuthbert in these words:

> 'This thorn remove
> And I will prove
> Your faithful friend to be.
> Relieve my pain
> And you will gain
> Wealth and prosperity.'

'I have no time to spend on you or the thorn,' said Cuthbert as he hurried on. He looked back but he saw no sign of the little man.

At last he came to the mountain. He began to climb. Three steps up. Two steps down. Three steps up. Two steps down. Three steps up. Two steps down. He continued to climb but being naturally lazy he had neither energy nor perseverance to continue the ascent. He was so lazy that he sat down on the mountain side but a puff of fairy wind came and sent him bumping, bumping, bumping down till he reached the base and fell into a stagnant pool.

He had no desire to go home. He went into the big world to seek his fortune. His friends heard of him no more.

A puff of fairy wind came and sent him bumping down

Conleth, the second son, waited for a long time for news of his brother.

'Mother,' he said one day, 'there is no sign of Cuthbert's return. I think I will go and try my luck at the fairy mountain.'

The mother baked a cake for him.

'Which will you have,' she said, 'the whole of it without my blessing or the half with my blessing?'

'Oh, hurry up and give me the whole cake.'

Conleth started off. His experience was exactly the same as his brother's.

He, too, went into the great world to seek his fortune. No news of him ever reached home.

Now Colman saw that his mother was very tired and that she had hardly enough to eat.

'Mother,' he said one day, 'I wonder would I have better luck than my brothers had if I tried to find the magic girdle.'

'Oh, *alanna*, what would I do without you? Still, I should not think of myself only. You might succeed and it would be a great delight to my poor old heart to see you rich and happy.'

Colman made up his mind to go and seek the treasure. He rose early the next morning.

The mother baked a cake for him to take with him on his journey.

'Now, *a mhic*,' she said as he was about to depart, 'which will you have, the half of the cake with my blessing or the whole of it without my blessing?'

'Oh, mother, *asthore*, I could not think of going away without your blessing.'

Colman started off. His mother stood at the door as he went away. She blessed him and blessed him till he came to a turn of the road and was hidden from her sight.

Then she went into the lonely house and cried as many other mothers have cried before and since.

Colman went bravely on. He came to the mound. The little man was sitting there. The pair of tiny shoes were beside him. He said these words:

> 'I ask of you good friend
> Your kindly aid to lend.
>   Do not refuse.
> Good luck and health you'll meet
> If on my weary feet
> You place these shoes.'

Colman answered: 'Indeed, my little man, I will gladly do as you ask.'

'Now,' said the little man, 'you deserve a reward for your kindness. Take these magic shoes,' he said, as he drew a pair from under his coat. 'Put them on when you come to the foot of the mountain. You will then be able to climb to the top without the least trouble.'

'Oh, thank you,' said Colman, 'that is a great reward for such small service.'

The little man replied: 'Small service can be true service and one good turn deserves another. Now I wish you a safe and pleasant journey.'

Colman looked back for a moment as he went on his way. The little man had disappeared.

He continued his journey till he came to the hillock.

Another little man was sitting there. The stick was near him.

He spoke these words:

> 'Oh! stranger hastening on your way
> A little moment kindly stay
>   To help me in my need.
> Good fortune then will come your way.
> Restore the stick to me I pray
> And great will be your meed.'

'Indeed, my little man, I will gladly do as you ask. It is a small service that you require.'

'Small service can be true service and he who gives gets. I will now bestow the stick on you. When you reach the top of the mountain a fierce, howling wolf will come towards you. Wave the stick three times and he will run in fear down the mountain.'

There was no sign of the little man when Colman looked back.

He continued his journey till he came to the thorn tree.

A little man was standing near the tree. He seemed to be trying to take a thorn out of his hand.

He said these words:

> 'This thorn remove
> And I will prove
>   Your faithful friend to be.
> Relieve my pain
> And you will gain
> Health and prosperity.'

'Of course, my little friend,' said Colman, 'I will try to ease your pain.'

With deft fingers he carefully removed the thorn.

'Now,' said the little man, 'here is the reward you will receive for your kind deed.'

'Indeed I do not deserve a reward for such small service.'

'Small service can be true service and can return to enrich the giver. Now take these,' continued the little man as he handed Colman a pair of strange looking gloves. 'There is a thorn bush growing on the top of the mountain. Put on these gloves and move the thorns aside and you will find the girdle.'

Colman thanked the little man and proceeded on his way. He looked back for a moment but the little man had vanished.

At last he reached the mountain. He put on the magic shoes and climbed to the summit without difficulty. Then the magic shoes vanished.

All at once he heard a fierce growl. He saw a huge wolf approaching. For a moment he was startled. Then he remembered the stick. He waved it three times. The wolf uttered loud cries and went howling down the mountain. The magic stick vanished.

Next he approached the furze bush. He put on the gloves which the fairy had given him and pushed aside the prickly branches. He came on a flat stone. This he lifted and there on a bed of soft moss was the precious girdle. The gloves had vanished when he pushed the thorn aside.

Colman placed the girdle inside his coat and hurried

down the mountain side. He was now worn out with hunger and fatigue but he struggled on bravely till he came within a short distance of a big house. He had almost reached it when his strength failed and he fell in a faint.

When he regained consciousness he found himself lying on a comfortable couch. A beautiful girl stood beside the couch and near her were her father and mother.

Brendan, the father, held the girdle in his hand.

'Please tell us your name,' he said.

'Colman is my name.'

'When you have rested and have had some food I shall ask you to tell us how this girdle came into your possession.'

After a time Brendan asked Colman to go with him to a room where Niav and Ita were waiting for them. Ita noticed his handsome face and manly bearing. She wondered at his poor clothes and felt that he must have known want and poverty.

'Now,' said Brendan, 'will you please tell us where you found this girdle. I may say at once that it belongs to this family.'

'I heard the story of the lost girdle from a strange man who came into our house one cold winter night. My two brothers set out to find it.'

'Did they find it?' asked Niav.

'No, and they never returned home. My mother is very poor. I determined to try to find the girdle so as to help her by gaining some of the reward.'

'You are a good son,' said Niav.

'How brave he is,' thought Ita.

'Having got my mother's blessing I started off to seek the treasure.'

'It is a wise son that seeks his mother's blessing,' said Niav.

Colman continued: 'Three little men whom I know were fairies made it possible for me to reach the place where the treasure was hidden.'

'Where is that place?' asked Brendan.

'The summit of the fairy mountain was the hiding place.'

'You know of the reward that is promised to the finder of the girdle,' said Brendan.

'Yes, but I wish to obtain only what will make my mother comfortable and happy.'

'How good and noble he is!' thought Ita.

'I think,' said Niav, 'that Colman should remain here with us for some time. We can send for his mother and arrange the terms of the reward.'

'A good idea,' Brendan agreed.

It was some days before Brid arrived. She had been ill and was unable to travel.

In the meantime Ita and Colman spent many hours together.

'I think,' said Niav to her husband, 'there will be little difficulty in settling the second part of the reward.'

'You mean about giving our daughter in marriage to the finder of the girdle.'

'Yes, I think they would both be pleased with that reward.'

'Well,' said Brendan, 'I would be happy to give my daughter to Colman.'

'I would be delighted to see them married,' said Niav. 'You know a good son makes a good husband.'

When Brid arrived all arrangements were made for a splendid wedding.

It took place amidst great rejoicing.

The magic girdle was the most prized of all their possessions for as both Colman and Ita often said, 'It was the girdle that brought us all the good luck.'

The Mountain Wolf

Long, long ago there lived among the mountains of Kerry a rich man named Brendan and his wife Cliona. They had three children, twin boys Ruairi and Fergus aged twelve years and Brian aged ten.

One day in early autumn the children were in the garden with Sheila, their nurse. Sheila had been nurse to their mother.

The boys loved her and she loved them. Brian was her special favourite, because he was particularly gentle and kind to her.

'Tell us a story, please, Sheila,' asked Ruairi.

'I think, boys, by this time you have heard all my stories.'

'But we like to hear them over again,' said Fergus.

'Well, what one will I tell you?'

The boys thought for a while. Then Brian said: 'Tell the one about the wolf.'

'Indeed I thought you were all tired of that but if you wish me to tell it, here it is:

'You have heard of the poor, lonely widow who lives in the little house beside the mill.'

'Yes,' came the chorus.

'Well, there is a sad story about her only child, Fiachra.

'One evening as darkness was coming on Fiachra was standing at the door of his house. An old hag came along. She was so strange looking, that Fiachra thought she could not belong to this world. Her black eyes glared at him. She drew back her large cloak and from under it a fierce wolf appeared. It snarled and growled. Fiachra was afraid it was about to attack him. He hit it with a stick which he had in his hand.

'The woman held back the wolf but turned to Fiachra and said: "Before the night falls you yourself will have the shape of the animal you would have hurt. You will never recover your own form, unless someone calls you by your name, Fiachra."

'A mist came over the boy's eyes. When it cleared both the hag and the wolf had disappeared.

'The spell, however, fell on poor Fiachra. When his mother came to the door to bring him in, he was not there. All she could see in the gathering darkness was a wolf hurrying towards the forest.

'The only one who saw what had happened was an old crippled man who sat near the house. He could not rise from his chair to call for help. It was from him I heard the story.'

'Where is he now?' asked Fergus.

'The old man died some months ago.'

'Poor Fiachra!' said Brian.

'Yes, poor lad, he has never been seen since, and all the wolves have gone from the forest, except one, which seems to have escaped from the hunters.'

'And the mother never found her son,' said Fergus.

'No, never, and she is a very sad old woman living all alone.'

Just then a messenger came to say that the boys were to go to their mother. She wanted them to go with her to the heather field.

Mother and children walked about the field for some time.

'Oh! look, Mother,' said Fergus. 'I have found a piece of white heather. That will bring me good luck.'

The mother laughed. 'Indeed, my boy, many people believe white heather brings good luck, but, white or purple, it is pleasant to see the heather bells stretching out over the field.'

Just then the mother uttered a sharp cry:

'Boys, there is a wasps' nest. Run from the field at once.'

The boys hurried out. The mother was the last to leave the field. A crowd of the wasps settled on her dress. When she reached home it was found she had been severely stung.

The doctor was sent for, but, by the time he arrived the poison had gone through her system. All kinds of remedies were tried, but the stings were so great and so numerous that poor Cliona lost the use of her limbs and it seemed as if she would never be able to walk again.

One day, about a year after the sad happening, the family were chatting together after lunch. Felim, a man from the garden came to tell them that Conn, the travelling man, had come to the house.

'Make him welcome,' said the father, 'the children love to hear his songs and stories.'

'May we go to him at once, Father?' asked Ruairi.

'Yes, of course. He will be as glad to see all of you as you will be to see him. I myself will come down later on. I wish your mother could come too.'

'Don't trouble about me,' said the mother. 'I am happy when all of you are enjoying yourselves.'

When the boys went into the kitchen they found Conn sitting at the table having a good meal. It was a pleasant meeting.

'Welcome, Conn,' was the greeting from all three. 'It is more than a year since you were here before.'

'You must have a lot to tell,' said Ruairi.

'Well, I have some news but, before I begin to talk, tell me about your parents.'

'Father will soon be here to see you, but poor mother cannot come,' said Fergus.

'I hope she is not ill,' said Conn.

The boys then told him all about the visit to the heather field and its sad result.

When the father came in, the old man almost cried as he said: 'I am broken hearted to hear that the kind mother has had such ill luck.'

'I know how sorry you are, Conn. The home is not the same happy place since she became ill.'

'Can no cure be found for her?' Conn asked.

'No. We have had the cleverest doctors that can be found, but no one can cure her.'

The old man was silent for a moment. Then he said: 'Wasp stings sometimes resist all human skill but I would not despair. There is a rare bush that grows on the side of a mountain near the forest. It has large purple berries. The juice from these berries when heated over a turf fire, is said to have wonderful healing power.'

'Could we possibly get these berries?' asked the father.

'Yes, but they must be collected by a relative of the patient.'

'Unfortunately,' said the father, 'I must leave home tonight and I will be absent for a couple of days, but I will try to get the berries immediately after I return.'

'Gathering the berries is not such an easy matter,' said Conn. 'There used to be many wolves in the forest.'

'Yes,' said Ruairi, 'but I heard they are all gone except one.'

'That is true, my boy,' said Conn, 'but that one is very watchful, and it would be dangerous for anyone to go near him.'

'Well, Conn, we will see what can be done when I return,' said the father. 'Enjoy yourselves now, boys, while you have your friends with you.'

The boys spent a very happy evening with Conn. He sang songs, played games with them, and told them stories.

From birth the twins had always slept in one room. Their beds, dresses and everything were of the same pattern.

After saying goodnight to Conn they went to their room and settled down for a talk.

'I think, Fergus,' said Ruairi, 'that you and I should go to the mountain and try to get the berries that would cure Mother.'

'But what about the wolf?' asked Fergus.

'I have thought of that, but perhaps we could avoid him if we slipped out after dark.'

'How could we find the berries in the dark?'

'We could take a lantern with us.'

'Indeed, Ruairi, I would do anything to cure poor Mother.'

'Well, we will steal out tomorrow night.'

'All right, Ruairi. I won't be a bit afraid and I know you are as brave as a lion. We won't tell anyone we are going. I am sure we will be able to get the berries.'

Next morning Ruairi told Fergus that he was sure they would succeed in their attempt to get the berries.

'I was dreaming all night that I had killed the wolf,' he said.

'We had better bring hatchets with us,' said Fergus.

That night the two boys left the house while everyone thought they were in bed.

They went quickly to the mountain. 'Let us go round to the side where the berries are,' said Ruairi.

With the hatchets held firmly on their shoulders, they marched bravely on. Just as they reached the bush they heard a snarl and, on looking towards the forest, they saw the wolf glaring at them.

At the sight, terror seized them. They dropped their hatchets and ran for their lives.

They had not been missed, but the next morning there was a great wonder among the workmen at the disappearance of the hatchets.

They told Brian of their adventure but warned him to keep it a secret.

Later in the day Brian was talking to Sheila.

'Conn has told us,' he said, 'that there are berries growing on the mountain that would cure Mother. All the wolves are gone from the forest except one. I wonder, Sheila, would that one be Fiachra.'

'Well, *alanna*,' said Sheila, 'if there was someone brave enough to go to the mountain and call out the name Fiachra, we would know if the boy is there in the form of a wolf.'

Brian thought things over. He determined to go to the mountain and call out the name.

That night Brian, instead of going to his room, slipped out quietly. He took the lantern with him.

When he reached the mountain he heard a snarl and saw the wolf coming out of the forest. He was terrified. His instinct was to run, but instead he called out the name, Fiachra.

Then in fear and terror he fell to the ground in a faint.

When he regained consciousness he saw a kindly face bending over him.

Two gentle arms helped to lift him to his feet.

'Oh! Who are you?' asked Brian.

'I am Fiachra,' was the reply.

'You have been under a cruel spell.'

'And you have broken the spell. When you called the name Fiachra, the form and nature of the wolf disappeared, and I can now go home to my poor mother.'

'You will have a happy meeting.'

'Yes, and I may thank you for our happiness. But why did you come here?'

'I was told there were berries on a bush which grows

When he saw the wolf coming he was terrified

on the side of the mountain. These berries are said to be a cure for wasp stings. Do you know where the bush is?'

'We will walk round the mountain and look,' said Fiachra.

When the boys found the bush, Brian wondered how he could bring the berries home.

He had forgotten to bring something in which to hold them.

'I have an idea,' said Fiachra. 'There is a tree in the forest that has enormous broad leaves. You can carry the berries on them.'

'While you, Fiachra, are getting the leaves I will begin to gather the berries. They must be gathered by someone who is related to the sufferer.'

With happy hearts the boys set out for home.

When they reached Brian's house they parted, promising to meet again to talk over their wonderful adventure.

It was late when Fiachra reached his home. His mother was sleeping near a window which looked out on the street.

Fiachra tapped at the window and said softly, 'Mother.'

The mother turned in her sleep but did not waken.

Again Fiachra knocked and called.

This time the mother sat up in bed.

'That was a strange dream,' she thought. 'I was sure I heard Fiachra's voice.'

Again Fiachra knocked and called.

This time the mother pulled back the curtain. Then she gave a cry and almost fainted.

'Mother,' cried Fiachra, 'open the door. Your own boy is home to you again.'

It would be difficult to describe the delight of the pair.

Fiachra was from that day the joy of his mother's heart and her strength and comfort in her old age.

In the meantime Brian knew that there would be someone in the kitchen till a late hour.

He left the berries outside the door and went in. He found Conn and Sheila sitting at the fire having a great chat.

'Oh! *avick*, I thought you were in bed hours ago.'

'Hush, Sheila. I have something to show you and Conn.'

He brought in the berries.

'These are the berries from the bush on the mountain,' said Conn.

'Yes, Conn.'

'How did you manage to get them?'

'I will tell you later on, Conn, but will you show me how they are to be used to cure Mother?'

Conn turned to Sheila and said:

'Get a three-legged pot, a little water from the well outside under the ash tree, and stew the berries over a turf fire.'

After some time, Conn said:

'Now put the juice into a basin and go and bathe the patient's feet.'

'Hurry, hurry, Sheila,' said Brian. 'We three will now go to Mother's room.'

Sheila was the first to enter the room. The mother was sitting at the fire, reading.

'Now, *achushla*,' said Sheila, 'it is time for you to be resting. I will bathe your feet and then you can go to bed.'

When Cliona put her feet into the basin she uttered a cry —

'Oh! what kind of water is this?' she said. 'My feet feel as they did before they lost their power.'

To her great joy she soon found she could walk again.

'What wonderful thing has brought about this cure?'

'Your son Brian may be thanked for it all. It was he who went to the forest and collected the berries which were the magic cure,' said Sheila proudly.

'But, Mother,' said Brian, 'it was Conn who told us about the berries.'

'That is true,' said Sheila, 'but you must tell your mother how brave you were, going to the mountain to face the fierce wolf.'

'But, Mother, Ruairi and Fergus went to the mountain, too, but they did not know what Sheila had told me.'

Sheila then gave an account of poor Fiachra's transformation.

'Well,' said Cliona, 'there are two very happy mothers tonight, myself and Fiachra's.

'Our suffering is now turned into great happiness. Indeed it was by the helpful knowledge and advice of Sheila and Conn that everything has come right.'

Cliona's Wave

A loud noise, as from the surging of a wave, is occasionally heard in the harbour of Glandore, County Cork, both in calm and stormy weather. It is the forerunner of the shifting of the wind to the north-west. It is called the 'Tonn Cliona' or Cliona's Wave and was supposed to portend the death of some great personage.

King Turlough and his Queen Sive had their palace near Glandore in County Cork. They were married many years and had no children. At last a beautiful baby girl was born. She was called Ethna and was the joy and pride of her parents' hearts.

One lovely day the king and queen were seated at a window in the palace, looking at the beautiful scene that lay before them.

> 'Cloudless sky and sparkling sea,
> Cliff and shore and forest tree,
> Glen and stream and mountain blue,
> Burst at once upon the view.'

'Who would not be happy,' said Turlough, 'while looking on such a scene?'

'Well, you and I are certainly very happy,' the queen

replied, 'and it is a joy to think that little Ethna is heiress to all this beauty. There she is, sleeping peacefully in her cradle under the hawthorn tree, with her faithful nurse by her side.'

'Sometimes,' said the king, 'I wonder if the nurse is so faithful. It has been whispered to me that she cares more about Fergus, the gardener, than she does about our little Ethna.'

'Oh, don't mind those idle rumours,' the queen said. 'I am sure she is very attentive to the child. Let us walk down to the sea. It is a pity to be indoors on such a day.'

'Look how calm the water is,' said the king. 'It is almost without a ripple, except where the wavelets break on the beach.'

'Yes, but there is a swell on the sea and the wind is turning to the north-west.'

Suddenly, a loud noise was heard, a noise as from the surging of a wave. Both Turlough and Sive trembled and turned pale.

'That is Cliona's Wave!' cried the king in great alarm.

'Yes,' said the queen, 'the wave that gives warning that some terrible sorrow is to come to us. Can we do nothing to lessen the fairy's power?'

'Alas no! No one is strong enough to lessen the power of the fairy, Cliona.'

They returned in haste to the palace. Everything there showed signs of trouble and confusion.

'Oh, what has happened?' cried the queen.

There was silence for a moment and then Turlough and Sive were told that their dear child was lost. The nurse had left the baby sleeping under the hawthorn tree and had gone some distance away to speak to the gardener. When she returned the child was gone. She had been stolen by the fairies.

'I knew,' said Turlough, 'that some great sorrow was coming to us when we heard the sound of Cliona's Wave.'

'Oh, why,' asked Sive, turning to the nurse, 'did you leave our child alone?'

'It is just as if she had died,' said the king, 'for we shall never see her again.'

From that time happiness and peace were gone from the palace. Sorrow and gloom reigned in their stead. Years went by without bringing any tidings of Ethna. Turlough and Sive tried to rule wisely and to look after the welfare of their subjects, but they never ceased to pine for the child they had lost.

One day Sive was walking along a road just outside the palace when she saw a woman and a little boy coming towards her. As the woman drew nearer, the queen saw that she looked very tired and ill. In a moment she had fallen to the ground. One of the queen's waiting women hurried into the palace to call for help. When the woman was brought in, it was found that she was dying. She whispered to the queen: 'My husband, who was a chieftain in a territory some miles east from here, was killed when defending his home from his enemies. I travelled here to ask you to befriend my little Donal when I am gone.'

In a few moments the woman was dead.

The queen felt it was her duty to take care of the little boy. Gradually she came to love him as if he were her own child. She and the king determined to make him their

heir. They often spoke to him of Ethna and it became the great wish of his heart to bring her back to her home.

Years passed and Donal grew to be a fine, handsome youth. He was as good as he was handsome. He had a great love of the sea and used to go many miles from land in a boat which the queen had given him. Sometimes he would take provisions with him and would spend hours on the water.

One warm August day when the sea was like a beautiful spreading lake under a blue sky, Donal ventured farther and farther from the shore. As he went southward, he saw in the distance a small island. It seemed to be covered with emeralds and rubies. As he drew nearer, he saw that rows of rowan trees grew round the coast. Their foliage and berries were what he had thought were gems glistening in the sunshine.

A little cove faced him as he approached the land. He made fast his boat and went in on the island. From the trees came the sound of human voices and, to his amazement, he found that these voices belonged to birds perched on the trees. Numbers of birds were there, brown, black, green and other colours, all chattering away in human speech.

While Donal was wondering at what he saw and heard, he noticed a strange-looking house in the centre of the island. It was built of stone and had a long, sloping roof.

The birds continued to talk. Donal lay down on the sward near the house and listened to them.

'Yesterday,' said the pigeon, 'I flew to Glandore Castle and rested in the hawthorn tree in the garden. The king and queen were sitting under the tree. They were

The voices belonged to birds perched on the trees

speaking sadly of the Princess Ethna who was carried away to fairyland many years ago.'

'They will never see the same Ethna again,' said the raven in a harsh, croaking voice. 'The fairy Cliona holds her a captive in her court.'

'Oh, you always have the worst news!' exclaimed the thrush.

'Well, I know what I am talking about,' retorted the raven.

'Peace, peace,' said the gentle voice of the dove.

'Yes,' said the little wren, 'let us be bright and cheerful.'

'Was Ethna the name of the princess?' asked the swallow from her nest under the roof of the house.

'Yes,' replied the pigeon, 'Ethna was her name.'

'Well, then I know where she is. In the spring, when we swallows were coming back to Ireland, we flew over a fairy fort some miles north of Glandore. I stopped to take a sip of water from a river near by. I saw a mortal maiden in the fort and heard the fairies call her Ethna.'

Just then Donal saw a boat approaching the island. An old, bent man came on shore.

'You are the first visitor that has come to my island home,' he said to Donal, 'and I bid you welcome.'

Donal thanked him and told him he had been much interested in listening to the conversation of the birds.

'Yes,' said the old man, 'these birds see and hear a great deal in their flights from the island and, as they have the gift of speech, they tell me everything that happens.'

'I have heard very important news from them,' said Donal.

'What is that news?'

'It is about the Princess Ethna, who was years ago taken from her father's home by the fairies. The birds say she is in Cliona's fort.'

The old man shook his head.

'Cliona has wonderful magic powers and, even if you could reach the fort, it would be difficult to rescue the princess. I can help you, however, if you are brave enough to attempt to bring Ethna back.'

'I would do anything to restore her to her parents.'

'Well, then I will give you all the help I can but there will be difficulties and hardships in your way. Cliona's fort is several miles north from Glandore. I will send the pigeon to be your guide by day and the owl to lead you at night.'

'But how will I know the place?' asked Donal.

'You will come to a great rock in the middle of a circular space. Round this rock is a row of smaller stones. This place is Carrig Cliona, that is Cliona's rock. It is useless to approach the fort by day. Wait for a moonlight night!'

'The moon is full at present and I should like to reach the fort tomorrow night.'

'You can do that if you return home now and set out in the morning.'

'I will take the fastest horse in the stable,' said Donal.

'No,' said the man, 'you must go on foot. When you have travelled about twenty miles, you will come to a little house half-hidden by trees. I will send one of my birds to tell the woman of the house to expect you.'

'But how shall I succeed in freeing Ethna from the fairy's spell?'

'That will not be easy. Cliona is very clever. She can take the form of different animals. She can become a deer, a hound or a rabbit but whatever shape she assumes, her green eyes remain the same. Before you set out on your journey tomorrow, cut a branch of the hawthorn tree in the palace garden, a branch with berries on it. If you can manage to strike Cliona with the branch, you will have her in your power and she must do as you wish.'

'And how shall I find Ethna?'

'Command Cliona to call her forth and the princess will gladly come. Do not on any account enter the fort yourself. You must not eat, drink nor speak from the time you leave the island till you reach the house among the trees. Now take my blessing and hasten away.'

As Donal sailed from the shore, the birds sang in a chorus:

> 'Happy will the princess be,
> When young Donal sets her free,
> He will break the cruel spell,
> And the fairy's power will quell.
> May kind fortune on him smile
> As he leaves our wooded isle.'

Everyone in the palace had retired to rest before Donal returned. The night was warm and he slept in a summer house in the garden. Early in the morning he went to the hawthorn tree to cut the berried branch. There, sitting on the top of the tree, was the pigeon which was to be his guide.

As Donal travelled on, the day became very hot and he felt tired, hungry and thirsty. He saw a woman coming towards him. She had a basket full of delicious fruit in one hand and a glass of mead in the other. She offered him the fruit and mead. Donal longed to take them but he remembered he must not speak, eat nor drink. He gave one longing look at the good things, shook his head and passed on.

When he had gone a little distance he looked back to the place where he had met the woman but she was nowhere to be seen, though that part of the road was quite straight, without bend or turning. The pigeon acted as his guide till he reached the house among the trees. Then the bird turned and flew southward. To his great surprise, he saw, standing at the door of the house, the woman who had offered him the food and drink.

'You are heartily welcome,' she said.

Donal thanked her and followed her into the house.

'You have bravely borne hunger, thirst and weariness,' said the woman, 'and now you will have your reward.'

She led Donal into the room where a delicious meal was prepared for him. When he had finished his meal she told him to go into the inner room.

'There is a bed,' she said, 'where you can rest till you hear the owl's cry.'

Donal was glad to rest and soon he fell into a deep sleep. He was awakened by the hooting of the owl. He went to the window and by the light of the moon saw the bird on the branch of a tree. As he was leaving the house, the woman said to him:

'If you succeed in your effort to free the princess, there will be food and rest for both of you here on your return journey. Take this horn,' she said, 'and blow it three times when you reach the fairy fort. Cliona will then appear before you.'

Donal again thanked the woman and followed in the direction in which the owl flitted from tree to tree. He came in sight of Cliona's rock. He blew the horn once, twice, three times. Out from the fort walked Cliona. She was very beautiful but there was a cruel gleam in her green eyes.

As she came near to where Donal stood, he attempted to strike her with the hawthorn branch. Immediately, she changed into a white rabbit and ran round and round the court. Then darkness fell. Donal felt something descend on his shoulder. It was the owl whose voice whispered in his ear:

'I will tell you when the rabbit is coming close to where you stand and will warn you when to strike...'

'Now,' said the owl, after a few seconds.

A piercing shriek was heard. The darkness cleared away and Cliona stood there, weeping and wringing her hands.

'Command the Princess Ethna to come forth,' said Donal.

'Come, Ethna, come,' called Cliona, as she herself disappeared into the fort.

From the centre of the court Ethna approached the surrounding rocks. She stepped outside and looked around her in wonder and joy.

'Oh,' she exclaimed, 'what a beautiful world! But where shall I find the loving friends I have so often seen in my dreams?'

'Come with me,' said Donal, 'and their joy will be

greater even than yours when you are all re-united.'

The owl led them back to the little house where the woman gave them a warm welcome. When they were departing on their homeward journey she said to them:

'There will be great rejoicing in the palace when you return and soon there will be a happy wedding there.'

The king and queen wept for joy when they saw their loved child again. Everyone in the palace shared in their delight.

The woman's words came true, for Donal and Ethna were married and lived happily ever after.

The Power of Music

Near the shores of Loch Corrib there lived centuries ago a chieftain named Aodan and his wife, Aisling.

They had been married many years and had no children.

It was a continual source of regret and disappointment to them that they had neither son nor daughter to inherit their wealth.

At last to their great delight a baby girl was born.

Everyone in the castle rejoiced from the chieftain himself to Balavaun, a poor deaf and dumb man who did odd jobs about the gardens and stables.

Egna, the chief's druid went out in the night to view the skies and read there what fate had in store for the child.

'Tell us,' said Aodan, 'what is destined for our beloved daughter?'

'She will be much loved,' said the druid.

'Oh, I am sure of that, but tell me more.'

'She will be clever and talented and music will play a large part in the happiness of her life.'

'Will sorrow or danger come near her?'

'Both will threaten but both will be averted, one by

devotion and love and the other by the power of music.'

'Tell me now, Egna, what name shall we give to the child?'

'There is one small star in the sky to-night which shines with special brilliance. The child should be named Reiltin (Little Star).'

At some distance from Aodan's house there lived a widow named Grania. She had one child, Conn, a boy about ten years old.

The news of Reiltin's birth did not bring joy to either mother or son. On the contrary it brought deep disappointment.

Conn's father had been a distant relation of Aodan and Grania had hoped that her son would inherit the chieftain's possessions.

'This is bad news for you, my child,' she said when Reiltin's birth was announced.

'I had hoped you would have inherited the castle and all that goes with it.'

'I had always hoped, Mother, to be the owner of that castle.'

'Well, my boy, don't be too much disheartened. I will see to it that you will yet be a rich man.'

Years passed. Reiltin had grown into a very beautiful girl. She was as good as she was beautiful.

There was one in the household whose affection for her was so great that he would make any sacrifice to give her a moment's joy.

This was Balavaun, the poor deaf and dumb man. In turn the gentle girl had the warmest friendship for him and repaid his devotion with kindness and consideration.

As the years passed a desire grew stronger and stronger in Grania's mind.

This was that she would bring about a marriage between Conn and Reiltin.

This achieved Conn would be at least part owner of the castle and all that went with it.

The mother and son were frequent visitors at the castle but Reiltin never even for a moment considered a marriage with Conn.

This was a bitter disappointment to him and his mother.

'Oh! if only that girl had never been born,' she would say, 'then you, my son, would have all the wealth which really should be yours. My heart aches for you. My own health is failing and you will be poor and lonely when I am gone.'

Conn grew to hate Reiltin even though he kept up a pretence of friendship for her.

Dark and bitter thoughts gathered in his mind.

'Oh! Mother,' he said one day, 'if only Reiltin could be got out of the way.'

'Hush, my son. Nothing can be done to secure what we had hoped for.'

One beautiful summer morning Reiltin went out alone. She walked by the bank of a river which hurried along on its way to the sea. On the far side of the road was a thick hedge.

In gladness of heart the lovely girl sang snatches of old songs as she stooped to gather flowers that grew at the water's edge.

By a strange coincidence Conn came along the road.

Reiltin did not see him and was quite unaware of his presence.

Suddenly a daring and cruel suggestion came into Conn's mind.

'There is no one in sight,' he thought. 'If she were carried away by the rushing river no one would know her fate.'

He crept stealthily towards her and was about to hurl her into the water when two strong arms grasped him. As he struggled to free himself he lost his footing. He fell headlong into the river and was carried swiftly towards the deep sea. Balavaun had followed his beloved mistress. He had kept behind the hedge on the far side of the road. When he saw Conn approaching he came noiselessly towards the river. He was just in time to save Reiltin.

The poor girl nearly fainted from the shock she had received.

Balavaun placed his arms round her and almost carried her home.

Her parents were terrified when they heard what had happened.

Aisling determined that she would never again allow her daughter to be alone. She would not feel easy, unless she or her husband was with her.

'But Aisling,' Aodan would say, 'Reiltin will never marry if you keep her always by your side.'

'Better that she should not marry than be in danger of taking a husband who would be unworthy of her.'

'You know, Aisling, many men have admired her. Any one of them would be proud to make her his wife.

Conn crept stealthily towards her

Your constant presence prevents any suitor from approaching her.'

'Well I refuse to relax my vigilance,' was the reply and so the matter ended.

Grania did not long survive her son.

She died almost immediately after hearing of his death.

After a time some guests arrived at the castle.

Among them was a young prince named Colm. He was accompanied by his harpist, Enda.

Colm was an only child. His parents had died when he was very young. Enda was his most faithful and best loved friend.

From the moment Colm saw Reiltin he felt that beyond all other women he would choose her for his wife.

In vain he sought opportunities to speak to her alone. Her mother was always by her side.

Reiltin, on her part, would have liked to speak to the gallant prince.

Colm thought things over.

'Enda,' he said to his friend the harpist, 'I wonder how I could have some conversation with Reiltin without her mother being present.'

'Let me think,' said Enda.

'Oh, yes. I have a plan.

'In your honour a great ball will be held in the castle tomorrow night. Reiltin's mother cannot insult you by refusing to allow her daughter to dance with the principal guest.

'I will play a tune for a dance in which the dancers change places. At the close those who have been at one end of the room will be at the other end when the music stops. You and Reiltin will be near the door by this time.'

'Is that the door that opens on the garden?' asked Colm.

'Yes. Then I will stop playing the dance tune and begin a *geantraighe* [a laughing tune]. All the company will begin to grin and titter and finally they will burst into riotous laughter. They will laugh and laugh till they become exhausted and will be forced to sit down and rest. You and Reiltin will fall under this spell.

'Then I will play a *suantraighe* [lullaby] which will cause everyone to yawn and nod and doze and eventually fall asleep.

'Balavaun will be hiding behind the curtains of the window which is nearest the garden door. He will not hear the music and will not be affected by it. Before you and Reiltin lose consciousness he will lead you outside into the garden. The rest of the company will be so drowsy that they will not notice your disappearance.'

'But how will you arrange all this with Balavaun? He cannot hear.'

'Sile, Reiltin's faithful maid, will by signs give him all necessary directions. She will place him behind the curtains before anyone comes into the ballroom.'

'Will he be sure to understand all he has to do?'

'Perfectly. Though he is deaf and dumb he is very intelligent.'

'Once out in the garden all sleep will disappear. Then you and Reiltin can arrange matters. I will continue the *suantraighe* for a short time. Then I will begin a *goltraighe* [weeping song].'

'What sort of air is that?'

'It is a weeping air. All the company will begin sighing and sobbing. Groans and lamentations will be heard on all sides.

'At the end of the *goltraighe* I will play three sharp, quick notes. These are the signal for you and Reiltin to enter the room.'

Next night the ballroom was a scene of great splendour.

Precious jewels and magnificent dresses added to the beauty of the scene.

After a time Colm asked if the harpist might play his magic music.

There was general assent to this request.

Enda, as already arranged with Colm, began to play a dance tune.

Colm bowed low before Aisling and asked permission to dance with her daughter. Aisling could not refuse the request.

The dance began. The music continued till Colm and Reiltin had reached the door leading to the garden.

Then Enda began to play the *geantraighe*. Smiles and grins appeared on every face. Giggling and tittering turned at last into peals of laughter. Everyone was forced to sit down, so tired were all.

Enda then began to play a *suantraighe*.

Gradually heads began to nod, eyes to close and after a short time nothing was to be heard in the room but loud snoring.

When Balavaun, peeping from behind the curtain, saw that the sleeping time had come he hurried out and drew Colm and Reiltin from the room. They were sleepy and dazed but the night air soon roused them to complete consciousness.

Then Enda changed the air to a *goltraighe*. Sighs and groans were heard on all sides. Weeping and wailing and lamentations filled all the room.

Aisling started up, wringing her hands and crying bitterly.

'Oh! my friends,' she called. 'Why are we all in tears? What is the cause?'

The only answer to this question was louder lamentation.

'Oh!' continued Aisling, 'where is my child? Where is Reiltin?'

Still louder wailing resounded through the room.

'Oh! where is Reiltin? If only I could find her I would grant her every wish.'

The music ceased and with it all the woe and weeping.

Then Enda struck three sharp notes.

Immediately the door at the far end of the hall opened and Colm and Reiltin entered.

'Oh! my child, my child, you are safe and well,' exclaimed Aisling.

'Yes, my dear,' said Aodan, 'and you can now as you have said grant her every wish.'

'What is it you most desire?' asked Aisling.

'Colm will tell you,' said Reiltin.

'I think,' said Aodan, 'I have known for some time what Colm desires, but I will let him speak for himself.'

'My speech will be short,' said Colm. 'I ask the hand of your daughter in marriage.'

Before either parent could speak there was a cry of joy and felicitation from all present.

'My consent is freely given and I think I can speak also for my wife,' said Aodan.

Poor Aisling was so much overcome by all that had happened she could do no more than nod her head in assent.

There was a magnificent wedding. The festival lasted for days and the last day was better than the first. All the people in the countryside shared in the joy of the happy pair.

Colm and Reiltin lived to a ripe old age.

They had many children and grandchildren.

Of all that attended on the families there was one who was specially loved. This was the faithful Balavaun.

As the years went by he loved Reiltin's children as he had loved their mother.

They learned to talk to him by signs and he was as a child among them.

He did not live to see the grandchildren but they were often told of the kind old man that loved Granny so much and of the way in which he saved her life.

'I believe,' said eight-year-old Colm to his twin brother Aodan, 'that Balavaun saved Granny's life.'

'Yes, indeed,' answered Aodan, 'and if he had not we would have no Granny now.'

The Stolen Treasures

In olden days there lived in a magnificent castle near the centre of Ireland a rich chieftain named Ruairi with his wife Manissa and their three sons, Sean, Aindreas and Brian.

There was another member of the household who was regarded as one of the family and who was loved by all.

This was Maire who had been nurse to the mother and afterwards to the three boys. She was very clever. Indeed it was believed she was friends with the fairies and knew some of their secret ways.

They were a happy family. Each of the sons had many precious possessions. Sean was a talented artist. Among all his work that which he treasured most was a picture of his parents which he had painted when he was quite young. Aindreas, a musician, was the owner of a splendid small harp. To Brian belonged a precious gold chain that had been in the possession of the families through centuries.

These treasures were kept among others on a large table in a room at the uppermost part of the house.

One lovely day in spring the family went to visit friends who lived at some distance from their home. They were to spend a few days with them. Maire accompanied them.

The other members of the staff were given a free time during their absence.

Great care was taken to secure all entrances to the castle against robbers or intruders of any kind.

At some distance from the castle there was a strange little house known as 'The Black Witch's Den'. It was situated on a narrow road remote from any other dwelling or building of any kind.

The witch, a small, thin, wizened old creature was the terror of the people for miles round. All in the neighbourhood were careful to bolt their doors when they had occasion to go from home.

It was said she cast cruel spells on anyone who came her way.

She saw with delight that the inmates of the castle were about to leave their home.

Oh! what treasure would now be hers! But how was she to gain an entrance to the castle?

She herself was the only one to find a way. At the back of the house on the top storey there was a large room. In it was a great wide chimney over a huge fireplace. The witch climbed up the side of the house by clinging to the thick, strong ivy that grew on the walls. By means of a rope she had taken with her she was able to descend through the wide chimney into a large grate.

She knew how to find the room where the treasures were stored. The bright, full moon shed its light through three large uncurtained windows.

Facing the light was a large table on which were placed many precious articles. Among these were the picture, the harp and the chain. The witch knew to whom they belonged. She hated the owners and their parents.

One by one she took the three treasures and placed them in a sort of handcart which she had left near the entrance to the castle. With cruel satisfaction she hastened to her den.

There was consternation in the castle when the family returned home.

'We shall never see our treasures again,' said Manissa.

'We all know it was The Black Witch who stole them and no one has ever recovered anything stolen by her.'

'Can you, Maire,' asked Ruairi, 'do anything to help us in this difficulty?'

'Let me think,' said Maire. 'The witch must have come down along the road that leads from her house to the castle.'

'But why should she travel along that long road when there is a short cut across the fields?' asked Manissa.

'Because,' said Maire, 'she would have had to cross the bridge over the river that flows along to the sea. We all know a witch cannot cross running water.'

'The case is hopeless,' said Manissa.

'No, it is not hopeless,' was Maire's reply, 'if we can get three people to undertake the work of restoring the treasures.'

'Could not our sons undertake this matter?' asked Ruairi.

'No, it must be done by three girls,' said Maire.

'But where shall we find these girls?' asked Manissa.

'We can find them,' said Maire, 'in a little hovel near the river. Their mother died about a year ago and the father did not long survive her. A cruel uncle claimed all that the girls possessed and left them homeless.'

'Send for the girls at once,' Ruairi ordered.

'By your leave, Master,' said Maire, 'we will send for the eldest first. If she is successful in restoring one of the treasures we can send for the second, and if she succeeds the third can go.'

'Well, Maire,' said Ruairi, 'you have always been so clever and faithful in looking after our affairs we will leave this matter entirely in your hands.'

'Will there be any reward for the return of the treasures?' asked Maire.

'Certainly there will. You say that at present these girls are living in a miserable hovel. If they succeed in restoring the treasures I will place them in a fine, comfortable dwelling. You know, Nurse, the house where my dear Uncle lived and died.'

'Yes, the one at a short distance from the castle.'

'Yes, now it has been vacant since my Uncle's death some months ago. It is a fine house and well furnished.'

'Indeed Master it is and the grounds and gardens are beautiful. They will be lucky girls if they possess such a lovely home.'

After this conversation Maire went to the hut which was now the home of the three girls Roisin, Emer and Ita. Three lovely girls they were. She told them about the robbery and of the reward that would be given for the return of the treasures.

'Will any of you girls undertake this adventure?' she asked.

'I will,' was the answer from three voices.

'Well now, girls, listen carefully to my instructions and follow them. You, Roisin, are the eldest and must take the treasure owned by the eldest son. It is a picture of his parents. Shortly after nightfall on the third night of the new moon, the witch comes out and walks round to the back of her house. She leaves the door open. Now when darkness comes on go towards the house. Hide behind the thick bushes which grow at a little distance in front of it. When the witch turns round to the side rush in and take the picture. She keeps it among other stolen articles on planks opposite her bed. They are to her a source of triumph. You will have plenty of light for she keeps the fire burning through day and night.'

Roisin found the next day very long. She waited till nightfall and then went towards the witch's dwelling. She hid behind the bushes.

After a while the witch came out and went round to the back of the house. Roisin rushed into the house. By the light of the fire she was able to see all the stolen things. She took the picture and hurried away.

She had scarcely left the house when the witch appeared. She saw the flying figure and immediately gave chase after it. Though she was old she was very fleet of foot.

Roisin heard her footsteps coming nearer and nearer but she managed to reach the river just in time.

The witch could not cross the running water. In rage and disappointment she returned to her den.

There was much rejoicing at the return of the picture. Roisin and Sean became great friends. Maire was delighted with the result of the adventure.

Roisin waited until nightfall then went towards the witch's dwelling and hid behind the bushes

'Now, Emer,' she said, 'will you undertake the task of restoring the second treasure?'

'Certainly, I will,' was the quick reply.

'You, Emer, have a lovely singing voice. The witch loves music. She can never resist listening to it. Wait till nightfall. Then go close to the door of the witch's den. Sing some of your sweetest melodies. She will ask you to go into the house and sing more. Begin by singing some funny, rollicking tunes, then one or two sad airs and lastly the fairy lullaby.'

Emer, like her sister, found the next day very long. She welcomed the approach of darkness and went to the witch's den. She stood near the door and began to sing some lovely airs.

Very soon the witch came out and asked her to go into the house and sing more. The witch seated herself in an old rocking chair and motioned to Emer to sit on the only other seat in the house, a rather rickety stool.

'Now please begin to sing,' she said.

Emer began by singing some lively airs with funny words. The witch laughed in delight. Then Emer turned to some rollicking dance tunes. The witch rocked to and fro to keep time with the music. Gently and slowly Emer began a sweet old Irish lullaby.

Gradually the witch began to nod. In a little while she had closed her eyes and was in a peaceful sleep.

Emer seized the harp and hurried from the hut. Congratulations on the success of her adventure greeted her on all sides. Some pleasant hours passed as she sang and Aindreas accompanied her on the harp.

When the time came for the restoration of the last

treasure Brian became greatly alarmed. He and Ita had become great friends.

'Oh! Ita,' he said, 'I fear there is much danger in attempting a third visit to the witch's house.'

'Now, Brian, why should I not be as brave and daring as my sisters have been? I am sure everything will be as well with me as it was with them.'

Though Ita spoke in that manner she was very anxious as to the way she could obtain an entrance to the witch's den. She determined to consult Maire, the old nurse.

'Now, listen, my dear,' said Maire. 'I have a key which will open any lock. Be very careful not to lose it as it is precious. Now, since your sisters have regained two treasures the witch is particularly careful to guard all her other possessions. Wait till after midnight when the witch is asleep. Open the door with this key. Take the chain and run.'

Ita followed all Maire's directions. She reached the witch's den at midnight. She had no difficulty in opening the door. The fire was blazing. She quite easily found the chain. Just as she was leaving the hut the chain rattled. Even that slight noise wakened the witch. She jumped from her bed and rushed after Ita. Closer and closer she came towards her. Just as both reached the bridge the witch stumbled over a large stone and fell headlong into the water. There had been heavy rain and storm during the day. The swollen river rushed on and bore her body far out to sea. Not long after all these stirring events there were three weddings and all concerned lived happily ever after. As the old storytellers say:

'They had children in basketfuls
Rocked them in cradlefuls
And if they don't live happily
That you and I may.'